GOT A GANGSTA CATCHIN' FEELINGS

PART THREE

A Novel by
Laconia Reneé

To submit a manuscript for our review,

email us at

submissions@majorkeypublishing.com

"For Cherita..."

PROLOGUE

NAS

Waking up and kissing my woman's head was like heaven on a Sunday. Whatever the fuck that meant. Making love to Camaya after she told me that we would be having another baby was bliss. There were a shit ton of changes that I was going to have to make, and I wasn't ashamed to make them. I knew that there was still trouble bubbling and boiling back in Jackson; especially with Donica. She could suck a mean dick and stay exactly where she was, because I wasn't too much concerned with her. I highly doubted that there was another chance that I would run into her anyway. What she did and said, when she brought what went down between us to light, it was over. Camaya didn't mention it.

I slid out of bed about an hour before she had to and grabbed my cellphone off the charging pad on the nightstand. Not yet checking it, I got Abby out of bed and got her ready for the day. Now that we were expecting another baby, I wanted Camaya to rest as much as possible before she had to go to New York for a show. That meant that I was going to have to pop a few whole grain waffles into the toaster, crack a couple of eggs and put them in the copper skillet for omelets. To my surprise, as soon as I pushed a spoon full of eggs into my mouth, my woman came around the corner in a black velour tracksuit.

She stopped in front of the refrigerator and scowled at me. "You turned my alarm clock off," she said with a raspy voice.

I nodded while chewing. Abby snickered in front of me.

"Nas, you made me think that I overslept."

"That wasn't the goal, but it was to let you get as much sleep as possible before you left."

She kissed Abby's cheek, then came over to me for a hug.

I got off the barstool and wrapped my arms around her

waist. "What's the matter, Cammy?" I grumbled.

Her shoulders hurdled. "Something is telling me not to leave. As soon as I leave, I feel like something is going to happen, baby. It's heavy on me. I've never had this feeling before."

"Work has to be done, babe. You can't just pull out of it. I'm sorry for putting us in this situation, but it's the way it is. I promise to completely cater to you when you get home. You takin' Lucy with you, aren't you?"

"Of course, Lucy's coming." Camaya laid her head against my ribcage and sighed. "I just have a really bad feeling, that's all. It's like if I go out there, something's going to happen to make me regret leaving."

"What would happen, though, babe?" I tightened my grip around her. "Abby and I are going to chill this weekend, spend some time, probably go to Build a Bear, and we're going to break all your rules. That's it."

She leaned back and slapped me across the chest.

I chuckled after getting a reaction out of her. "Seriously, baby, nothing is going to happen that's not supposed to happen. Now, you sit here and eat while I go and bring down your luggage."

"Okay," she said with a pout.

Softly, I grazed my hand over her stomach before leaving. I couldn't wait to see my unborn again, but her next appointment wasn't for another three weeks. To know that I'd be a father by blood now, it was something that had me floating on air. My life was already complete when Abby came into the world, swinging and screaming. I remembered holding her for the first time, shaking like a sinner in church. She made me fall in love faster than I did with Camaya. I vowed to always keep her safe and to love her, no matter what life threw at us. I could only wonder if my reaction would be the same with the new baby. It was too early to tell what the sex was of it just yet, but I was praying for a boy.

Camaya wouldn't stop kissing me and Abby when her Uber driver had arrived. That bad feeling she had just wouldn't go away, but I needed her not to stress for the sake of her health and for the baby. My sweetheart wasn't going to listen though. I sent her a text almost an hour later, assuming that she had already made it through TSA. She replied with a quickness, just to remind me that she loved me and Abby.

If I had it my way, and we had nothing to lose, I would've convinced her to stay at home. Unfortunately, I had errands to run. Abby and I had to go to Trader Joe's just to get some organic junk so we could lounge around and watch Peppa Pig, and I could play Call of Duty on my Xbox One, all the while she had a controller that didn't have a battery pack in it. I loved spending time with my little woman. Abby brought so much joy to me that it was almost unbelievable.

"I want chocolate pretzels, Daddy!" she announced once I got out of the car.

Opening the back door with a smile, I promised, "I know, baby. We'll get your pretzels."

While unbuckling my daughter, I could feel a presence behind me. Sharply I turned, finding a brother about two feet behind me in a full suit and bowtie. He pulled a smile across his face as he approached me with a pamphlet in his hand. "As-salāmu ʿalaykum, my brother."

I scanned him closely, returning, "Walaikum salaam."

"Oh, so you belong to the Nation?" he asked hopefully.

"Nah, my brother. It ain't like that. I just know the greeting."

"Oh, okay. So, are you looking to start a journey—"

"I'm not lookin' to do anything besides get my daughter inside of this store before she throws a fit over her snacks."

"Maybe you should stop by." He handed me the pamphlet that I didn't even care to look at. I just took it to get him to give me some space. "We have a garden of our own. Your princess would love it there. She could grow her own fruits while learning the science and nature of things from true aggies."

"Thanks. You take care."

"You too."

I didn't watch him walk away. Instead, I tossed the pamphlet over onto the back-passenger's seat and finished unstrapping Abby.

Later that night, I was playing the game after cleaning Abby's mouth. One look over at her and I had realized that she was out of it. She couldn't hang past nine o'clock. With a chuckle, I turned my head toward the TV in the game room. Then, my phone blared a familiar ringtone that jolted my daughter out of her sleep. It was Conz's ringtone.

Quickly, I snatched it up and answered for him. "What's good?"

"Bruh..."

CHAPTER 1

LAZ

When I had everything said and done, Donica wasn't happy at all. I was able to get a lawyer who had my shit sealed. She threw one hell of a fit about it all, but that was her problem, not mine. She eventually took the money without having to go to court. That meant that I was the happiest broke motherfucker anybody would ever see. With my house up for sale and me maintaining a small apartment, I was content. That was until I got the phone call that shook everybody. Having Meech to reach out to me about something other than work, had my head in the toilet. Everything happened so fast that it was almost impossible to catch it.

I cleaned myself up, got myself together, and drove to the house on Woodland Circle. Sitting in my car for a second, I had become upset. There was still so much I wanted to prove to Puff. So much I wanted to say. So much I felt I needed to do. He wasn't there anymore. I pulled my trusty canteen out of my glove compartment and opened it. So badly I wanted to take a sniff. Then again, I thought of what Puff might've said if he saw me or knew of me getting my nose dirty.

With a heavy heart and head, I ventured into the house. It was deathly quiet. Big Bruiser, Puff's bodyguard that always stood on his left side, wasn't at the door or in the foyer. It was confirmation that this moment was real. He was really gone. The sitting room on my left was filled with the big wigs and their top earners. It meant that if Meech had called me here, I had gone up the tier to being one of the best sellers in the league.

Meech took his arm across his nose as he sat in Puff's favorite tall-back chair, and Jamilla rubbed each of his arms. Before I could even get to the stairs, Nas was coming down with my daughter on his arm. My throat had locked.

Nas stopped directly in front of me and stared me down. "He didn't make it to that island," he said with a

16

shaking voice. "We're going to have a memorial and then fly his body out. Do you agree?"

He was asking me for a vote? I must've really been able to have a seat at the table if I was asked for my opinion. Apparently, I had come far when pushing myself to the limit that I hadn't even noticed. "Yea," I returned with the same volume. "It's what he would've wanted."

Lightly nodding, he turned away from me and went to find an empty seat on one of Puff's long couches.

"Daddy," Abby said with a very light voice. She held his cheeks in both hands so he could look into her eyes. "Why are you sad?"

"Well... Somebody very important went back home to God, and I'm going to miss them very much."

"Is Papa Puff not really sleeping?"

Sadly, Nas shook his head.

"God will send him back, right?"

"No, baby."

"Why? Why did he have to go back home to God?"

"It's how it works, Abby. God sends you here through your mommy's tummy. Then, you enjoy and experience everything that he has in store for you. When he thinks you're done, he calls you back home, and it only looks like you're sleeping."

"So, I won't ever see him again?"

"No, baby."

Abby hugged Nas's neck as she let out a little sniffle. It broke my heart twice, because I felt that she should've been mine. That should've been me having to explain life and death to her.

If my day couldn't get any worse, Camaya passed me in her leggings and a long white tank top. She went to Nas, where he stood to hug her with his free arm.

"I got here as soon as I could," she told him. "I knew that I shouldn't have gone. I had a bad feeling in my stomach."

"Did you check in and whatnot?"

"Yes, baby. Everything is taken care of. I have two days before I have to get back. Don't worry about that."

18

"Meechie?" Jamilla softly called Meech. She bent at the waist and kissed his ear. Meech was taking Puff's loss harder than anyone else. "Meech? You want to step outside?"

He shook his head though his cheeks were sopping wet.

"Y'all, the coroner is here," Conz announced from behind me. "Everybody got to say their goodbye's, right?"

"I didn't," Camaya said. "It's okay. Let them do what they need to do. I'm sure that we'll be going to the funeral home before the memorial. It's fine. I'll do it in private."

I moved out of the way to let the two people who came from the funeral home take the stretcher upstairs. It wasn't long before they came back down. The vibe had shifted in the room. My heart was shattering with every second that my eyes lay upon the black bag they put Puff in. It was way too late for me to be a man and to prove so much to him. While I looked on, I could hear the women finally break. Wails and calls soared through the house. Suddenly, a thud caught my attention, just as the workers had closed the back doors to their van. I turned to look inside the sitting room. Camaya was holding Abby, and Nas and Conz were trying to get Meech off the floor. All Jamilla could do was cry. It looked like he was having a seizure. He was that upset to where he had put himself in epileptic shock.

Quickly, I moved through the sitting room and kneeled beside Conz so that we could turn Meech over onto his side. From the looks of it, nobody had ever dealt with someone who was epileptic before. I had to grab a napkin off the coffee table to temporarily stuff into his mouth so that I could get whatever saliva was there to avoid him choking. Afterward, I pulled my phone out of my back pocket to call emergency assistance before he could swallow his tongue. Meech was twitching hard and flinching as if he was possessed.

Luckily, Puff lived in a good neighborhood. The first responders arrived in less than five minutes, and we had to help them to get Meech on the flat board. It was a scene for the ages, but I was glad that I could help, because they would've lost him had I not known how to handle that situation.

"Thank you," Jamilla said to me. She threw her arms around my neck before skipping out of the door to be with her dude.

Strangely, Nas patted my back before he left out of the door with his little family in tow. I couldn't even watch them leave. Shit, I had to wait until Conz had gotten into his car before I went back to my spot. It was there, when I was alone, that I broke completely. I needed to get a hold of my life, and it was sad that it took for a man to die in order for me to see that he only wanted his employees to better themselves. I only wished that I could've done that shit a long time ago instead of fuckin' around. I would've had a gorgeous wife who would be there for me. I would have a beautiful little girl who would look at me with a gleam in her eye as if I was the most glorious thing to see. Hell, I would have real friends instead of a posse that was only around when I was on or throwing a party. To do a justice to Puff, in his memory, and for my-damn-self, I was taking that road.

MEECH

I didn't know what the fuck had happened. All I knew was that one second, I was trying to hold in my cries, and the next, I woke up in an ambulance with Milla crying over me. Now, she paced at the foot of my hospital bed, working her neck and pointing her damn finger. I rolled my eyes at her. I knew her better than I knew my-damn-self. She was mad because she loved a nigga, but she couldn't bring herself to say it. Especially not after the way I turned my back on her after she had gotten rid of our kid. For the last two and a half months we had been meeting up in secret, smashing and dashing. Neither of us had brought it to the other's attention that we were still in love.

"Milla, why is you still yappin' at the man?" Conz asked her from the couch on the far-left wall. "He look like he don't even understand what the fuck you *yapp-a-gatin'*."

"You stay out of it!" she lashed at him. "I know Michael-Angelo can understand what I'm saying."

"Sit down, girl. We done had one hell of a morning—
"

"I'll sit down when I'm done complainin'! Now you shut it before you make me forget where I was!"

I took a deep breath. "You were at the part where I finally said that I love you and forgive you."

"Right! Your motherfuckin' ass—" Milla had to shut the fuck up and take a step back for a minute after she had snapped. Slowly, she brought her hands up to her mouth as tears formed in her eyes. "What?"

"We were at the part where I was saying that I didn't want to live without you anymore. Where I was tired of playin' like I couldn't stand you, all because you were lookin' out for your future. Where I told you that I wouldn't love nobody like I loved you. And we were at the part where you stopped cryin' and brought your loud mouth ass over here to hug and kiss me like you meant it."

"Meech," she whined. "You mean it?"

"Yes. Does it look like I would be fuckin' with you right now? I just lost my father and had a seizure when I

23

didn't even know I was able to do that shit. Stop cryin' and come over here, Jamilla. I need that hug more than you know."

Her mean ass wore a scowl as she stomped over to me and threw her arms around my torso, and laid a kiss on my lips that I had requested. It felt good to have a genuine side of her after so long. I mean, the only thing that made us come together in the first place was Camaya. We had to look after her while Nas was settin' shit up in Cali. Then came Abby. Uncle and Auntie's baby. We would stand to be in the same room, just for them. Having to go years like that, we were kind of diggin' each other again. I remembered how fine as fuck she was and she remembered how good the dick was. We could play like we didn't miss each other outside of the sex we had, but we each knew the truth. There was only one woman for Michael-Angelo Taylor, just like it was only one man for Jamilla Clark. In six years, we were single as fuck. I only fucked hoes and sent them away. From what I had heard, Jamilla dated, but it wasn't nothin' serious.

"Ain't that cute?" Camaya asked with a smile in her

voice.

Finally, I was able to break our kiss. I didn't even realize that we were still kissing. Jamilla had that strong effect on me. She could lift me up and have my head so far off into the clouds that I didn't realize it.

"That's not cute, Abby," Conz told her. "You don't ever want a boy to kiss you, okay? And if they try, you lay him flat on his motherfu—"

"Conz," Camaya hissed.

"You come tell Uncle, okay? Kissing is nasty."

"So, what is this?" Nas asked. "Is this a reunion, or…?"

"Shit, it might as well be. Milla don't talk to no other niggas, and Meech really don't give a second thought to no other female."

"What you say, Conz? Like… three or four months and we'll be ring shoppin'?"

"Two and a half weeks."

"Bet money."

Conz reached into his wallet and pulled out two $100

bills.

Nas matched his. I smacked my lips and shook my head. "How are y'all gon' bet on me, man? Y'all are supposed to support me."

"I'm *is*," Conz laughed. "I'm supportin' your relationship right on over to my bank account."

"Oh, baby!" Nas gasped. "You wanna kind of lighten the mood?"

Camaya scrunched her brows for a second until she caught on to what he was saying. "Oh! Right! So, you guys… Abby's going to be a sister!"

"Hell naw!" I screamed.

Jamilla slapped my arm. "Where's your wallet? I want my money, Meech! I told you!"

"Come on, Nas! I thought you were going to wait until y'all were married!"

"Fuck all that. Where is your wallet?"

"I don't have it on me, babe."

"Okay, well, give me the password and email to your

account. I'll transfer it over. It is still your first and last name, eight-o-two for the email?"

"Hold on," Camaya giggled. "Y'all bet on me being pregnant?"

"We damn sure did. I told this fool that you had a glow when you were out here last. He argued me down that Nas was takin' precaution because he so-called knew his bro. I put money on it."

"I can't believe y'all."

"Well, believe it. We even bet that Abby was really going to turn out to be a boy."

"Guys!"

A tender knock came to my door. We didn't know who it could've been since I didn't have any family and we just sent Puff on home. The last person I had expected to see came inching into the room with her Jordan's making no noise against the floor. She was dressed in a pair of tight jeans and a leather jacket that stopped just above her hips. Fashionably, she flipped her hair over her shoulder and got a good look at me on the bed.

"Why the fuck are you here?" Jamilla asked her. "Please don't make me act a fool in front of the baby."

Donica removed her shades and plastered a smile on her beat face. "I was just coming to check on Meech, is all. He is family."

"He ain't got no family. Especially not you."

"Why so hostile, Jamilla? I'm just being nice."

"We don't need your niceness. But since you're here and you want to be so kind, how about you repeat what you said about my homie Cam?"

"Excuse me?" She nervously giggled.

"What's wrong? You need a refresher? That coke get to you? You called her fat and said that Nas was beggin' you for a baby? Girl, I don't know why you're here and I'm sure that you don't even know right now. Get the fuck out."

Donica took a deep breath as she replaced her shades. "Meechie, get yourself checked, alright?"

"What?" Me and Milla asked in unison.

"I wanted to tell you in private, but since your girl over here has a mouth that can't be tamed, then that'll shut her up. I'll bring you back what you left in my car another time."

Jamilla lunged for Donica but thank God that Camaya was closest to her and grabbed her.

"We understand that you're not happy with your own life," Camaya said, "but comin' around here to stir up everybody else is only gonna end horribly for you. Go and bother your husband. We don't care. Just leave. This was completely random and irrelevant."

"Y'all don't get it, do you?"

"Whatever point you're trying to make needs to be made immediately, because I don't want any fighting around my daughter, and I won't be able to hold Jamilla for long."

"You think you got it made, huh? Camaya, I sacrificed this man. Had it not been for me stepping aside, you wouldn't have had him. And Jamilla? Girl, while Meech ain't busy hittin' you, he's callin' my line drunk and bangin' me. Conz can attest to that. He's had a taste too."

29

"Good for you. You're the group's groupie. We applaud you for your honesty, now leave."

"Lastly, when are you going to tell the girl that my husband is her father?"

"Never, because her father is holding her. Now, leave."

"Whatever. Your fat ass ain't worth my time. I'll holla at Nas later."

"Please," Camaya said. "I want you to try."

"Try what, Fat Albert?"

Camaya let go of Jamilla, but my baby had to look back at me. The tension in the room grew thick as hell. Everything shifted. Camaya approached Donica and backhanded the fuck out of her.

"Now try to sue me," Camaya dared her. "I want you to. And if you think of hittin' my husband's line, that little slap you got will be the least of your worries. Get the fuck out of here, with your miserable ass."

Donica was in shock. So much in shock that she couldn't take her eyes off of Camaya as she backed out of the room.

"I knew it was comin'," Conz stated calmly. "It was only a matter of time before somebody put their hands on that hoe. Don't come in here and try to *negativitate*."

Camaya went to Nas and grabbed Abby out of his lap. She was whispering some sweet things to explain why she hit Donica and reminded her that hitting is wrong. I admired how she parented, but it just made me feel like I wouldn't have that chance because Milla and I were so different.

"You ain't gon' ask me if it's true?" I asked Jamilla, who was now sitting in the chair beside my bed.

She shrugged. "She's a hoe and you were single. I don't need to ask."

"I'm talkin' about the disease part."

"You think that I give a fuck about what she said? Meech, if you had somethin' then I would too. But on short notice, we're back together as of this very minute. If I so much as see that dog anywhere near you—"

"You won't."

Conz burst into laughter. "I'm trying to figure out why

she targeted you, Meech. I fucked her too, so if you had somethin' then I would too."

"I don't know, dawg. Fuck that girl. She's probably mad at the fact that Laz divorced her, so she wants to make everybody else miserable."

"He did it for real?"

"Hell yea. Gave her fifty stacks to keep her distance."

"Damn, I could've helped him get money out of her. I got pictures and texts in my phone. That's infidelity. Easy win in divorce court."

"Nah. His head so far off into the clouds and he's been so quiet and to himself, that I'm pretty sure he don't even care right now."

"Michael-Angelo, I don't trust her," Jamilla said. "I feel like she's gonna try some shit."

"Don't even worry about her," I told her. "We'll be up out of Jackson after this memorial. This is the shit that I was talkin' about, Milla. I didn't want to come back here for a reason. Ain't shit left for us in Jackson. This motherfucker got bad vibes through and through."

"I know, baby. We'll be gone soon."

"Shit, I hate to admit it," Conz chimed in, "but you right, Meech. It's like, when I landed in ATL... I felt free. It was some sort of liberation, like the land that I stepped on was mine. Like everything that I was about to do was meant for me. The only good memories that I have of Jackson are with y'all. After that, I can't remember what good thing happened to me by myself."

Camaya shook her head. "I told Nas the same thing; that it's like Jackson is cursed. I couldn't stay here those whole two weeks. Even though I had to work, I dreaded coming back."

"Shit, Cam. You had it worse than any one of us. I can see why you didn't want to come back. On some real shit though, with the way we have everything worked out... after this memorial, we don't have to come back. It ain't shit here for us. The only way I'm comin' back to Mississippi is if I'm comin' to see Milla and Meech. But, shit, that's all the way up there in Columbus. I don't want to come back here, dawg. I can't."

"Look, Meechie," Jamilla offered. "I'll sign over the

33

shop. It's safe to say that we all agree. This bitch gives me a really bad feeling that I can't shake. I'm gonna have to put eyes on her. She's a little too bold to be walkin' off into hospital room, throwin' some random shit around."

"I know, baby." I reached over and grabbed her hand. Jamilla was always rock-steady, which is one of the reasons I loved her, so for her to start to panic, it was something that needed to be looked into.

CHAPTER 2

CAMAYA

Never had I lied to Nas. Heading back to take care of my business was one thing, but to lie to him was another. I loved him too much to do so, so it never left my lips until last night as I was packing to get ready for my departure. I told him that my flight landed three hours after the time it was supposed to. It gave me a window to do something that I had no business doing. In my rental, I drove to Laz's mom's home. He wasn't there, and she told me where he lived. I knocked on the door in hopes that he wasn't out being a hoodlum. Had it not been for me erasing his number out of my phone, I wouldn't have to drive like a bat out of hell or wear a hood and shades so that no one would recognize me.

My heart was pounding after I knocked on the door. I was scared that Laz would either scream when he saw me or send me on my way. Eventually, the door opened, and he stood there without a shirt on. His wide eyes and raised brow let me know that he was puzzled as hell as to why I was at his home.

"We need to talk," I informed him. "Do you have a minute?"

He stood there for a moment, weighing his options. Then, he peeked out of the door to make sure I was alone. Afterward, he stepped back inside the house and allowed me entrance.

Laz waited until I took a seat on his nice black leather couch before he opened his mouth. "I would say something nice and casual, but considering as how crazy your man is, I just want to know what this is about? Why are you dressed like you came to rob me?"

I placed my handbag next to me and clasped my fingers together. "Laz, listen, Donica showed up the other day at the hospital. We didn't know what she wanted, but she started spitting really recklessly to everybody. One thing in particular she said that hit us all was that Meech needed to get checked for something. His bloodwork came back

36

clean, but it worried me. According to her, she's run through Conz and Nas too. They say she's on cocaine, so I was just wanting to know if you were okay. The girl's out of her mind. Even Jamilla doesn't trust her. She just seems like making everyone else unhappy is a priority, and if you married and divorced her, then you're on the hit list too."

"Thank you for worrying about me, Camaya, but I'm fine. She has a restraining order."

"That's just a piece of paper. What if she comes over here welding a gun in her hand? Is it going to be able to protect you?"

"You got to forgive me for my nonchalant attitude when just a few months ago, you ran away from me. Now you're in my apartment, trying to warn me about a crazy bitch that I know already." Slowly he moved over to his coffee table and took a seat on the edge. "Camaya, this girl won't stop until everybody else is beneath her. Her being on cocaine is the only real news there, because I've never known her to use it. I mean, I've heard rumors like everyone else. Not once have I seen her do it. Your best bet is just to go back home where she can't hurt you, your family, or your career. I'll be fine."

"Laz, she's crazy. If she can stare down a whole group of people and—"

"I assure you. I will be fine. Y'all just need to go home and carry on like she doesn't exist."

"Laz—"

"I know that this is hard for you to do, but you have to trust me. You got to dig deep and find some kind of trust. When the memorial is over, go home and forget about Jackson."

I took a deep breath and stood off the couch with my purse in my hand. "Tomorrow evening, Nas will be working. Meet me at the entrance of LeFleur's Bluff State Park. I'll have a special gift for you." Before he could even ask me what it was that I was giving him and why, I reached around him for a hug that he wasn't at all expecting.

Laz sucked in a shaky breath as his arms nervously curved around my waist. "I'm so sorry for what I did to you, Camaya," he whispered.

"I know. I forgive you. But Laz, you're going to have to forgive yourself. I'm fine and so is Abby. We both live and eat pretty good. She's in a very good school, she's perfectly healthy, and she's spoiled rotten." I pulled back to look up at him, inside his red and puffy eyes. "Be at LeFleur's Bluff State Park, okay? This is going to be our final goodbye. And whatever you do, don't tell anybody. If it gets back to Nas, he won't be happy."

He lightly nodded with a bowed head, whereas I let myself out. Almost as if he could feel that I was lying, Nas sent me a text that scared the daylights out of me.

"Headed to the barber with Conz. Abby wanted to stay with Milla and Meech. When you get in, that's where I'll be. It's crowded, so I'll be here most likely until you land. I love you, babe."

I couldn't reply to it because, technically, I was still on my plane. To waste time, I did something that I never thought I would. Since we were leaving Jackson and never coming back, I decided to go to the Horizon Apartment Complex. My hands shook on the steering wheel after I parked, and I felt as though something was squeezing my

39

lungs. How would I face my last demon before I left? I didn't know but I had to.

A short, round woman answered the door to my old apartment. One who recognized me right off. She told me that my mother had moved in with my aunt down the street over a year ago. She was only fortunate to get the apartment that we had since the complex had remodeled it. Soon, I found myself at 147 Wildwood Circle, Jackson, Mississippi. It was my aunt's house. She was supposed to be my only hope. We saw how that went when she easily took my mother's side and believed her when she said that I was out being fast. At least, I thought she did. I never contacted her to see if she would be my escape.

Nervously, I knocked on the door in hopes that someone would answer and that the drama wouldn't pop off so soon. The woman who answered the door was as thin as rails and had a bruise on her cheek. It broke my heart right off. To think that she was getting the same medicine that she served me almost made me happy, but it hurt me nonetheless.

"Mama," I barely mumbled. "What happened to your

face?"

"What are you doing here?" she returned with narrowed eyes. "I thought you killed yourself."

Was she serious? "No. Obviously not, because I'm standing right in front of you. Where is my aunt?"

"She died a few months back and left me the house. What you want? Money? I ain't got that. Lookin' at how you're dressed, you don't need none of that no way."

"Who's at the door?" a man yelled.

I almost flinched at his voice, except I was used to Nas blowing a gasket or two.

My mama bowed her head in shame at this sound of this man's voice. "Nobody," she hollered. When she looked up at me, there was a shimmer in her eye that told me she needed help. Whoever this man was, he was doing this to her.

"Then close that goddamn door!"

"I'll be back," I promised her. "Have whatever you need packed, because I'll be back."

"I can't go nowhere with you," she whispered with misty eyes. "He ain't gon' let me leave."

"Ha! You haven't had the chance to meet your son-in-law. I promise you that you'll be able to leave."

As I took a step back, she threw her arms desperately around my shoulders for a squeeze. Maybe she would thank me aloud for helping her. Maybe one day she would even say that she loved me.

———————

Casually I strolled into the barbershop to see my baby. I had so much to tell him that I didn't know how I would get it all out.

"What's hannin', Cam?" Conz greeted me from his seat against the wall.

I threw a smile and wave his way after I spotted my monster. To my surprise, his face was bare. My jaw slid open as I approached Nasir in shock. "Baby," I whined. "What did you do?"

He chuckled while his favorite barber finished his 360-wave taper fade. "I had to get rid of it, baby. You don't like my clean shave?"

I playfully scratched at his thin mustache that he kept. Without his beard, my baby had a baby face. "It'll grow on me, I guess."

"What're you doin' here so early?"

"Hmm? What?" How could I forget that I was keeping to a certain time? That was completely stupid, and it's only going to come back and bite me in the ass. "Oh! My flight? I landed early."

Nas squinted at me. Simultaneously, he moved his hand from underneath his plastic tunic. In his hand was a black, velvet box. "I got you something today."

I took it from his hand with a smile, hoping to recover from the lie I had almost choked on. After I opened the box, I saw that it was a diamond encrusted butterfly. My smile grew as I stared at it. He knew that I loved butterflies.

"Yea, I thought that would make you grin after the hard work you put in."

I gave it back to him so that he could take it out of the box and place it onto my middle finger on my right hand.

He easily slipped it onto my finger and kissed it.

Moments later, we were walking up the steps to Meech's apartment, ready to get Abby and go back home. While we waited for one of the love birds to come to the door, I had to burst out with what was wrong with me in the first place.

"Nas, I went to see my mama," I confessed.

His brows squeezed with his eyes prying into mine. My baby was so confused that I might as well had thrown an English book in his face and told him to write me an essay on Shakespeare.

"I came home early, had some time on my hands, and went to see her. She lives in my aunt's old house with some guy who's likely beating her. I saw the bruise—"

"Say no more," he cut me off. "When are we going to put his ass out?"

"Maybe tonight. I'm not sure."

The door was opened by Jamilla. She had a large smile on her face. "Y'all might as well leave Abby here. She's asleep. We'll keep her for the night. Besides, she's the only thing to cheer Meech up out of all of this. Lord knows I've tried."

"Fine," Nas grunted. "Look, y'all can't hold my daughter hostage forever."

"Boy, shut up. As long as you're here, I might as well. Y'all go and enjoy each other." With that, she shut the door in our faces.

"Babe," I mumbled. "Did she really just withhold our child from us?"

"Mmhhmm. But I know what we can do to pass the time." Nas took me by the hand and escorted me to my car.

We ended up going to the old house, where we shook the walls with our love-making. It wasn't until my fourth orgasm that I realized, for me to get pregnant in the first place, Nas didn't wear a condom. Any other time we made love, because he knew that we weren't ready for kids, he would wear a condom, regardless if I was on birth control or not.

"You sonofabitch!" I yelled, slapping his chest. Then, I climbed off of him and stared at him on the bed for a moment.

"Babe, what the fuck?"

"You trapped me, Nas!"

"Cammy, what are you talking about?"

"You got me pregnant on purpose, didn't you?"

"I'm still lost as fuck!"

"We have always been protected because I didn't want more than Abby until my career slowed down a little bit. You've always been strapped! We can't get pregnant while wearing a condom, Nasir! You were bare! Admit it!"

Slowly, he dragged his hand down his face. He had been caught, and there was no way that he could admit that he wasn't. "Listen, baby," he grumbled. "We've moved past the whole 'I like to have my way' thing, alright? That was then, and this is now. Besides, I thought that you were still taking birth control. I wasn't thinking about having another baby. I came home, saw you, got excited, and here we are. I can't help that I'm sexually attracted to the woman I want to make my wife."

"How many more times are you going to put me in a

situation that I can't control? Do you honestly think that it's fair?"

"No, I don't."

"Then, why do you do it?"

Nas got off the bed and headed into his old master bath to run the water inside the shower.

"Excuse me? I need an answer from you."

"It's because I'm a control freak!" he bellowed with his eyes hard on me. "Camaya, some things are hard to change, okay? I'm trying, here. You knew what it was when you stepped into it. I don't want to hear shit else about it!"

"Says the control freak."

"You want to have a go? We can argue all night long if you want, but we're going to have to do it over the phone, because I have to work."

"Like always."

"You gon' keep doin' that? For every-fucking-thing I say, you gon' have a remark for it?"

I rolled my eyes as I snatched my robe down from the closet door. Slipping it on, I said, "I'll bathe in the hall bathroom. It's just funny to me how you can control every-damn-thing, leaving me with no say so in any matter."

"Why are we going over this?"

"Because you have a problem that you need to adjust. You didn't even stop to think about how much traveling I was going to do while being pregnant. Granted the fact that I'm keeping the baby, it's still the fucked up part that you didn't think about me in all of this."

That was my exit. I could do what I needed to, so I could meet with Laz. Although I was being honest with everything I said, it was still an opportunity for me to tell no more lies, yet leave him there to think about what he did.

CHAPTER 3

CAMAYA

Talk about being a nervous wreck. I kept checking my phone to make sure that no one was trying to call. Nas had only sent a text apologizing, but that was about it. I had retrieved Abby from Meech's and didn't explain why Nas wasn't with me. My stomach churned at the thought of them contacting him, and him throwing a fit when trying to figure out where we were.

Soon, I pulled into a parking space where I saw a nice luxury car already there. Nervously, I got out and walked over to the car, where the door had opened, and Laz stepped out. He was comfortably dressed in a white v-neck and a pair of creased jeans. Without him knowing what to expect, I threw my arms around his shoulders to make him feel a little more comfortable.

When he pulled back, he looked at me as if I had grown two heads. Slowly, I backed away until I hit the back-passenger side door, then pulled it open. Carefully, I unstrapped my daughter and let her out of her car seat. I could hear the harsh escape of breath that rushed from his lips. It was like the wind had been knocked out of him.

"Abby, I want you to meet someone, and I want you to be nice," I said. With a wide and gentle hand, I softly pushed her toward Laz.

He squatted and ran his hand down his face, I guess to try and contain his tears.

Abby clutched her doll at her chest and looked up at him. "Why are you crying?" she asked sweetly.

Laz shook his head for a moment. I could tell that he was trying his best not to break. "Because," he choked. "You're so pretty."

"Thank you. Who are you?"

He licked his lips and looked down at the pavement to ready his answer. "I'm nobody. Just an old friend of your mom."

"Oh. I like your necklace." She reached out and touched his diamond and gold cross. "My daddy has one like this."

"Well, how about we give it to the doll." Laz took off his necklace and draped it around her doll's neck, then kissed the doll's forehead. "I think it looks good on her."

"It's big!"

"It is, isn't it? Listen, you be a good girl, okay? I want you to be sweet, and smart, and outgoing. I want you to be the best at everything you do. Can you do that for me?"

She animatedly nodded, but the screech of tires made us all flinch.

I turned at the sight of lights, wondering what the hell was going on. A black SUV was mere inches away from my car, while a black Cadillac swerved in front of the SUV to block the back of Laz's car.

Nas jumped out of the Caddy with his Jesus piece swinging wildly at his chest. His eyes were those of a mad man. "Get my wife's car and take it back to the house," he ordered a man behind me. He then picked Abby up off her feet and took her to his car. After strapping her in, he mugged the hell out of me. "Get in the car, Camaya. I don't want to repeat myself or act an ass in front of my daughter. And you?" When he set his sights on Laz, I could've sworn that he was about to kill him. "I told you, didn't I? You better thank the Lord that Meech sees something in you."

"What?" Laz asked.

"Go see Meech. Your ass should've been working with us instead of coming to see my wife."

"Nas, I—" I started.

He cut me off with a look that told me that I had better keep my mouth shut and get my ass in the car before he lost his cool for real.

I took one last look at Laz that told him how sorry I was for having to leave him behind. I should've known better than to sneak behind Nas's back. He had eyes everywhere.

Still, I got inside the car where Abby had already popped in a DVD so she could watch her cartoon on the screen inside her daddy's headrest. I couldn't hear what

Nas was saying to Laz, but that was the least of my worries. When Nas got in, he looked back at Abby and smiled, then pulled away from the lot.

Almost ten minutes of silence and we pulled over into a vacant lot. This wasn't good. He dug around in the armrest for a moment, and then got out of the car to open Abby's door. He then plugged in a set of headphones and handed them to her. "Stay in the car, baby. We'll be right back."

"Okay, Daddy," she happily replied.

He closed the door, traveled over to my side, then opened my door, unbuckled my seatbelt, and grabbed my hand to pull me out. My heart was racing. Nas only hit me once, but something told me that he was bound to do it again today.

I stood against the back of the car with my hands clasped together, waiting to hear how he knew where I was.

"You lied to me," he said angrily. "Your fuckin' flight landed at noon, Camaya!"

Oh shit!

"You have *never* lied to me!"

"I can explain—"

"No need to. I know where the fuck you were. I checked the fuckin' GPS! What the fuck were you thinking?"

"Nas—"

"You went to see this nigga, and then you went back to your old projects, and then you made another stop. I knew somethin' was off with you. You accused me of cheating on you twice! Never have I, but you got the nerve to lie to me? I trusted you, Camaya!"

"I didn't cheat!"

"Then explain yourself! Why did you have my daughter around this motherfucker? Hmm? *Explain!*"

"I thought that it would put him at peace!" I cried. "I felt bad for him, Nas. How would you feel if somebody else was raising your child and you had to sit back and watch?"

"That wouldn't happen because I would never throw my kid away!"

"Stop screaming at me!"

"Woman…" he said a little calmer, but the anger was still there. "You don't need to feel bad for a nigga who was voted to take on the duties of Mississippi because of his fire, his determination, and his vigor. Lazarus has this whole fuckin' state to worry about now. Abby should've been the least of his worries."

"And how would you feel if your baby's mama's new man said some shit like that?"

"He threw her the fuck away; don't you understand that? I don't give a fuck how badly he misses her, or how bad you felt for him. Why was I not consulted with this decision?"

"When the hell am I ever consulted when you want to do something?"

Nas had finally shut his trap. He actually took a step back to think about everything for a second.

"All you ever do is make decisions without me and

then persuade me to do what you want. Well this is a decision that Camaya made on her own, Nasir. I thought it was best before we leave, because he would never see her again. Yes, I have feelings, and yes, I care about people, no matter how badly they have treated me. The bottom line is that he created a life. Maybe he's not raising her, and no, Abby doesn't even know his name. But he created her, and I felt that it was fair for him to at least speak to her. I don't want her growing up with regrets. I don't want her to see him on the street in the future and wonder who the hell he is because they look so much alike. Maybe you weren't built to feel certain emotions, but I was." During my rant, I couldn't help the tears that cascaded down my cheeks. I was so tired of screaming without being heard. It was ridiculous and redundant now. "Excuse me for being softer than you, or taking other people's feelings into consideration, but that's just who I am."

"Baby—"

"I'm tired of doing this with you! We argue, I end up the one who isn't heard, then I'm hurt, and I still have to only see your point or do things your way. I'm not doing that anymore, goddammit! I made my own decision and you will deal with it!"

"Camaya, listen!"

I threw my hand up and tried to go back to my side of the car, but Nas had blocked my path and grabbed my shoulders. It was a struggle for a moment for me to set myself free, yet the more I wiggled and squirmed, the tighter his grip had become.

"Baby, stop!" He shook me a little, but I couldn't bring myself to look him in the face. "I didn't want Abby to be confused, alright?"

"I didn't confuse her! She doesn't even know his name! All he said was that he was nobody when she asked who he was."

He backed up a little with a softer grip at my arms. "He said that?" he asked in disbelief.

"He did. Then he told her that he wanted her to be the best at everything. Not everything is malicious or confusing. You would've known that had you decided to listen to me instead of yelling and making it all about you."

Finally, I pushed him off of me and wiped my tears away. "I did what was right. I don't care if you don't see it that way. We *all* get it, and we understand you're her father. Hell, even Abby told him that you were her dad when she complimented his necklace. Everything doesn't have to be a push and drag match with you."

"Baby, I'm sorry."

"I'm tired of hearing that. That's your strike two. The next time, you won't have a choice but to sign those fuckin' papers, the way that *I* want things done." With that, I went to my side of the car and snatched the door open.

I didn't understand why getting my point across had to be so dramatic with Nasir. Hopefully he could change soon. Hell, hopefully, we wouldn't have this problem when we got back to Calabasas. I didn't want to tear my family apart, but if I had to hurt myself and explain a confusing situation to my daughter, just to be happy, then so be it.

CHAPTER 4

NAS

Camaya was pissed at me. I swear I was working on my anger and my overreacting. It just seemed that every step I took was the wrong one. I looked over at her in the passenger seat as I drove, wondering when the hell she was going to look at me.

"Baby," I called her with my eyes on the road. "You gon' give me the address to your mama's?"

"It's already in the GPS, Nasir," she grumbled.

"Baby... I said I was sorry. I mean, I know you're tired of hearing me say it, but it's true. Work with me, Cam, damn. You act like I dragged you, cheated on you, abused you, and popped up with other bitches and babies. This shit still new to me. Five years, Camaya. We've been together for almost five years. Do you blame me for not ever noticin' how much of a control freak I am? You're the one who has the house all set up when I come home. I don't have to put my luggage and shit up because you do it. I don't have to make a drink or cook dinner, because you do that too. Laundry? You do that shit too. Forgive me because I'm spoiled as fuck. I'm tryin' to adjust, alright? You already put your foot down with me, and I understand that, but baby, I was hurt and shocked. First you pull a knife on me, then you threaten me. Afterward, you left me in Jackson, and then you drew up paperwork. For you to lie to me… how else am I supposed to react?"

"Nas… Just… Drive."

"Nah, fuck that. I have a point. Shit's changing, and since I'm spoiled as fuck and I'm used to bein' a boss, I don't like change."

"That's what you do as a couple. You grow together."

"Well then fuckin' grow with me and stop being mad at me. I just want you to work with me, baby."

She only shifted in her seat without looking at me.

I knew my Cammy. I knew what would make her smile

and what would bring her out of that mood she was in. Playfully, I flicked her titty through her shirt.

"Quit," she whined.

I poked her thigh then, getting swatted in return. So, I pinched her nipple and ducked out of the way before she could hit me.

"Nas, I swear to God," she giggled.

I exited off the freeway and waited until I reached the stop sign to lean over and peck her cheek. She knew she couldn't stay mad at me.

"You play too much," she complained through a laugh.

"You know I love you, girl."

"I love you too," she returned with a sigh.

I couldn't help but to grab her chin, turn it toward me, and kiss her full on the lips. Our tongues tangled for a while, while an erection grew in my jeans. I had to break the connection because I was there to see about her mama; not take her into a dark alley and bend her ass over.

Camaya took a moment to get herself together before

she spoke. "You know that I wouldn't want you to be a savage at times, but I'm afraid that this situation calls for you to be yourself."

"What you mean?" My brows squeezed. We had just had an entire conversation about my anger and shit.

"I mean that I don't know this guy, but my sweet demeanor and patience won't do anything for him. He yelled at my mama to close the door, babe. She has a big ass purple bruise on the side of her face. I don't know if you've ever seen my mama, but she's a little darker than me. You would have to hit her pretty hard to leave something on her face like that."

"Don't worry about it, baby. You just stay in the car, and I'll handle old boy. Do you trust me?"

"Yes."

"Alright then."

Moments later, I parked on the street, right in front of a small one-story house that looked like it needed some serious work. I kissed Camaya's cheek and took one look at my daughter in the backseat. Abby had finally gone to sleep. Her schedule called for it, because it was after 9 o'clock.

Finally, I got out of the car and went up to the door. I prayed that I wouldn't have to use my heater that was tucked under my shirt. I banged on the door instead of knocked. That would get somebody's attention. Hopefully it would be the nigga who decided to put his hands on my mother-in-law.

The door swung open and a dude that was at least three inches taller than me answered without a shirt. The mug on his Teflon colored face told me that he was down for whatever at that moment. "Who the fuck is you? Why the fuck you knockin' on my goddamn door like you're the fuckin' police?"

"Oooh, you should've been a little more nice to me when you greeted me." I sucker-punched him dead square in the forehead. As soon as he fell on his ass, I took my knee across his face to lay his ass out. Then, I stepped over him so I could find the bedroom. At this time of night, that's the only place that my mother-in-law should've been. "Ms. Webber?" I asked, as I entered the master bedroom. She wasn't in there. I backed up a little and turned the knob on the door at my right side. After turning on the light, I saw her sitting in the corner of the empty room that smelled like piss so badly that I had to turn my head momentarily. "Ms. Webber?"

"Who are you?" she asked me with a shaky voice.

"I'm Nas. I'm your son-in-law. We came to take you home."

"I can't leave," she cried. "He'll find me—"

"Let his ass try, and I'll handle him. Get up and come with me."

"He out there?"

"Passed the fuck out. Come on. This room is burning my eyes, which is why I can't look at you right now."

I didn't know if she had gotten up until I felt the door open a little wider. She inched out of the room, looking around the hall as if that fat, black fuck was going to dash out of one of the rooms at any given moment. With a quickness, she darted into the master bedroom, grabbed her purse and phone, then jetted down the hall. I took my time to go behind her, wondering what the hell was going on in that house.

Camaya got out of the car when she saw her mother. Meanwhile, I dragged the fat fucker away from the door so that I could close it behind me. Cammy put her mother in the backseat as I approached the car, and got in. There was nothing that came out of my mouth just yet, but I knew that as soon as we got to the house, I was going to hear it from my wife.

I tucked Abby in and kissed her forehead before turning off her bedroom light. Camaya's mama stood in the doorway to watch us parent our sleeping child. Thank God that she had showered and changed into a pair of Cammy's leggings and tank top.

"Daddy," Abby whined sleepily. "My light."

"Your nightlight is on, baby," I returned quietly.

She turned over in bed and clutched Peppa.

Together, the three of us traveled into the dining room where I poured up a glass of brandy for myself and one for my mother-in-law. I knew she needed one with the way she was shaking. Then, I made my baby a glass of iced tea.

"Camaya, you should've forgotten about me," her mother said. "He's gonna come lookin'—"

"And Nas is not afraid to deal with him," Camaya countered.

"Y'all seem like a pretty good family. I don't want y'all mixed up into my problems."

"It ain't no mix-up," I said as I sat and placed the glasses in front of the appropriate person. "You're still family after what you did a few years back."

"I'm sorry, who are you again?"

"Mama, this is Nasir Asaad," Camaya introduced me. "He was basically my savior after everything went down when I was pregnant with Abby. He's my boyfriend."

"Her *husband*," I corrected her. "With me, you don't have a reason to be afraid of anything, alright? Fuck him and whoever else he feels like bringing with him. My name puts fear in the hearts of many. Long story short, he doesn't stand a chance at getting you back, so you might as well make yourself comfortable. We leave for California tomorrow night."

"California?" her mother hissed. "I can't go all the way out to California, Nasir."

"You can't, or you won't? The way I see it, you don't have a choice. This man had you locked in a pissy ass room. What the fuck were you doing in there anyway?"

"What?" Camaya screeched.

"That's my sister's house," her mother pleaded. "She left it to *me*."

"Then we will take the route for proper protocol and have him legally evicted. We'll fix it up and put it on the market to put money in your pocket. In the meantime, you're coming home with us, and nothing you can say or do can tell me otherwise."

"Camaya, I cannot leave."

"Fortunately for you, you weren't put out in the cold with your ashes for clothes in the parking lot." Camaya pushed away from the table and went inside the office to work. I noticed that she had done that, even when there were other situations to deal with.

"Vanessa, you really fucked that up," her mother whispered to herself.

"Take a drink," I prompted her.

She did so, damn near guzzling half her glass.

"You know, my wife is very soft-hearted. She sees what is fair and just. For you to reject her after she set out to save you after what you've done, it really hurt her feelings."

"What am I supposed to do?"

"Make yourself comfortable and get ready to move to California. In the morning, before we leave for a memorial, just have a chat with her to try and mend the past." To outdo her, I drank my entire glass, then wiped my mouth clean with the back of my hand. "See you in the morning, Ma Nessa. While we're gone, you're going to have to shop for a few outfits and shit."

"Nas, I can't take your money."

"You and your daughter with this opposing me shit. You'll learn how she did. It's either you shop for yourself,

68

or I send someone to do it for you." I got up from the table and went into my room to get ready for bed. Before I got into the shower, I placed my phone on the charger and sent a text to a wicked witch, even though I didn't want to.

"I'm coming by tomorrow. Be at home all day. Don't make me come and look for you. We've gone long enough without speaking to one another. It's time we sit and chat. I have people I want you to meet. Specifically, my wife and daughter. You better hope this line ain't disconnected."

I waited about five minutes for her to reply. Anger rose within me. She had better reply before I made that phone call.

"Timothy?" she replied.

"You already know. And my name is Nasir. I told you that when I changed it."

"I don't give a fuck what you named yourself. I know what I named you and that's what I'm going to call you."

"Like I said, be at home all day so you can meet my wife and daughter."

"You don't run shit, Tim."

69

"It's Nas, and you read what the fuck I said. Don't be home and it's on."

"I'm not scared of you or your threats. Bring it on, baby boy. I was a G before you, and I'm still on now. It's where you get your G status from, or did you forget? So, what's up? Your move."

"I love you, mama."

"I love you, too. I'll be here after Puff's memorial. I guess I'll see you there."

"Bet."

"Goodnight."

I took a deep breath and went into the bathroom to take a nice, long look in the mirror. If I wanted better without the bullshit of Jackson, I needed to close out every chapter and mend every wound. Even if that meant scratching the scab off of my and my mother's damaged relationship. Abby needed to meet her family. All of them. Thinking of that, I shook my head at what I was about to do. I went back into the room and grabbed my phone again to send yet another text that I hoped I wouldn't regret.

LAZ

Meech opened the door with a scowl, then stepped aside to let me in. He got right down to the business so fast that he didn't even let me sit on the couch.

"Here's the thing," he said coldly. "With the way we got everything worked out, some of our top sellers are moving to our cities, understand? That leaves you and six others here in Jackson. You're the veteran. You've tagged along enough and you know enough about the business. You're the only one who knows about the shipping schedules, who's going to be bringing what, and you know how to work the hell out of the books. You were chosen to stay behind and hold Jackson down. Now, I fought for this, because you know damn well that Nas doesn't give two shits about you. Fact of the matter is, you came up under him. You need to move like he moved and work how he worked. I know you got it in you. That's the bottom line. Don't let me down, because I was the only nigga rootin' for you."

I had to back up a bit and shut my eyes tight to make sure that what he had said was actually what he had said. "You mean to tell me that I'm a boss?"

"You've always been one. You just moved up the ladder."

"Hold on, Meech. You're telling me that I have to run Jackson."

"Nigga, do you want me to spell it out for you? Yes! You're a big wig now. That means that when me, Nas, and Conz come together to have meetings, you'll be at the table. We have one the night after tomorrow, so pay attention to your phone. I'll let you know where it is and what time. You want to make a good impression, be early."

He didn't even let me thank him before he basically pushed me out of the door and sent me on my way. Still, I didn't see how I deserved to sit at the table with them. When I got to my car and checked my bank account, I almost passed out in my driver's seat. A motherfucker was workin' so hard and so much that I didn't notice how much extra money I had. Shit, whatever magic it was, I needed to repeat that shit.

73

Just after I pushed the button to the ignition, I got a text from Nas. All it said was, "We need to talk." I didn't know what the fuck was going on, but hopefully nothing could put a limp in my step. Something I was doing was finally paying off.

I pulled up to Nas's old spot and looked at my glove compartment. Nah, I didn't need my canteen anymore. Whatever he had to say would only be taken with a grain of salt. Cautiously, I strolled up to the door and knocked. He opened it with his phone up to his ear, wearing no shirt, and only pajama bottoms.

Casually, he gave me an upwards nod to enter. I did so, with the quietness of his home grinding against my ears. It was nearing ten at night, and for me to be inside his home meant that this must've been important. He finger-gestured for me to follow him down the hall. As I followed, my heart sank into my knees. I didn't hear not a TV, murmur or snore. We stopped in front of an open doorway, where he had extended his arm inside. Nervously, I leaned in to see that the room had a glow of different shapes of colors twirling around the walls. It was from the covering of a nightlight that spun from the socket. The moons and stars cast upon the sweet, chubby face that I had seen an hour and a half prior. Abby slept so peacefully with Peppa Pig at her side. Her hair was taken down from her thick afro puff that Camaya had it in. She looked so angelic, even in the dark.

I didn't know how long I was standing there, and I had been so lost in my thoughts that when Nas tapped my arm, I shut my eyes to snap out of whatever trance I had been in. He nodded toward the end of the hall for me to follow him. Then, we ventured down the long hall and down the stairs, where the door on our left opened. Camaya stood there in a pair of short tennis shorts, suffocating tank top, and a pair of glasses. The look on her face would've led you to believe that she was caught doing something that she wasn't supposed to be doing.

She pushed her small rectangular frames up and ran her hand over her silk scarf. "What—"

"Needed to have a man to man," Nas quietly explained. "Mama sleep?"

Camaya slightly nodded.

"Good. I'll be right back."

"Nas—"

"It's alright, babe. I'm calm, cool, and I have no reason to be upset. I promise. We're just going to have a little talk. Get ready for bed. I'll be back in about thirty minutes."

Her eyes darted over to me for a second. She was still as confused as I was.

"You done working for the night?" he asked her.

"For now, yes."

"Alright, my little work-a-holic. I'll see you in a minute." He leaned down and over to kiss what little of her forehead had been exposed.

I gulped, wondering what this talk could've been about.

We made one stop in the kitchen, where he grabbed an old tin domino can and tucked it under his arm. Once we made it outside, he placed the can on the wooden rail and opened it. Then, he handed me a fresh blunt along with a wooden match. Shit, I fired it up to put my own nerves at ease. I still wanted to know what this man to man was about.

Nas inhaled and held his smoke for a moment. As he let the smoke out of his mouth, he said, with a raspy voice, "I'll give Camaya three minutes at the most to realize that I don't have on any shoes."

"What?" I asked confusingly.

Sure enough, the patio door slid open and she placed his Venetian slippers at his feet. Without saying a word, she went back into the house, leaving us out on the patio.

Nas lightly chuckled as he slid his feet inside his slippers. "You know, no matter if she's mad at me, uncomfortable, or busy, she never forgets to take care of me."

I looked at him strangely. Our so-called man to man couldn't have possibly been him rubbing shit in my face.

"Yea. She's a good homemaker too. Neither of us would've known that unless we gave her chance. See, I fell in love with Camaya by accident. I thought that I was just

77

helping her out of a bad situation, but it turned out that while I was away in Cali and she was still here, that I couldn't wait to stop workin' so I could get back home to video chat with her. I mean, we rarely said a thing to each other, but we felt the same thing. Shit, we were scared to say what it was out loud. Then Abby came along. I was a nervous wreck when Camaya was pushing. I was wondering if Abby would recognize my voice from when I would speak to her when Camaya would read to her in the womb. I wondered if she would see what a malicious man I was. I wondered, right then and there, if me being perfect was going to be good enough for her. I wanted to know, at the same time, if I could manage giving her the universe along with everything her little heart desired. Laz, I was shaking so badly that it was the first time anyone would see me afraid. No kid wants to see Clark Kent, you know? They see daddy as Superman. From the first time I was able to hold her in my arms, I had vowed that I would always be her Superman. I would protect her from any and everything. So you see, when I rolled up on you, I was being a darker version of Superman. I didn't want her to wind up confused or hurt. I was angry that Camaya went behind my back to introduce you to my daughter. It took that same woman to drill into my head that it was only fair for my daughter to know the man who created her, even if she didn't know who you were. It's also the reason that I invited you here, so you could see her.

"Every night, we gather as a family and pray, and she *must* have her Pig. Without it, all hell would break loose. She's also a dancer. She hates dance class, but she's a pretty good dancer. I didn't want you as a part of her life, but it caused so much stress when we finally came back to Jackson. Especially a lot of stress on Camaya. I love that woman with everything in me. I just didn't realize that I was practically dragging her along and putting so much on her with my grudge toward you. In the event, I denied you the right to see or get to know the life you created, even if you showed out and denounced her and her mother. It's funny that we think just because we make money and handle some tough decisions in the street that we're men. That's not what makes us men. What makes us men is when we can swallow our pride and get rid of our fuckin' egos to make the best decisions for our families. That includes bowing down to our women and giving in to what they want. Now, after the memorial in the morning, we're going to pack the rest of our shit and get the fuck out of here so we can head back to the Hills. I want you here to say goodbye to Abby. I'll step aside and allow you the rest of the time with her before we leave. That way, you won't go through life without knowing or experiencing who she is."

"Thank you," I mumbled.

He placed his blunt at his lips and nodded. "Just be here right after dinner. I'll be done explained to her who you really are and why you'll be here."

"Hey, can I ask you a question?"

"Might as well, while I'm in a giving mood."

"What made you vote for me to takeover Jackson? What did I do?"

Nas choked on the smoke from his blunt through a laugh. "You serious?"

"Yes." My brows raised. I didn't see what was so amusing.

"Nigga, you know how much I put on your plate when

Puff called us out here for that itinerary?"

"Yea?"

"Yea, well. You soared through that shit. I expected you to fail, but you didn't. You did more than rose to the occasion. You know how much money you brought in? Shit, you had Meech recountin' shit, starin' at the books, askin' people if they saw you actually workin', and scratchin' his head. Even when you set up your college fund and somebody won that shit, and the check cleared. You're a king, nigga. Get used to it. That's why you were chosen. You proved that you could get your back up off the wall and do what needs to be done. Oh, yea." He reached into the pocket of his black and red, plaid pajamas and brought out a bank roll. "Finally, you went forty percent over your quota. Three times, actually. This here is your bonus. It's from me, Meech, and Conz. Congratulations."

Cautiously, I took the roll into my hand. I wanted to pass out at all the love and good news, but I couldn't show this savage a weak side. He was once my boss a few hours ago, and now I was able to say that I was sitting next to him at the table of Kings.

"Now, if you will excuse me, I need to get to my woman before she comes out here and demands that I come to bed. Speaking of my woman. Laz, I know you feel like you fucked up, which you did, but you don't have to stalk her to prove a point. You just need to forgive yourself. I need you to do that before tomorrow evening, because I don't want you to be tore up in front of my kid. Abby will ask you every question in the book. She's inquisitive like that." He tapped my arm, put out his blunt, then went back inside the house.

My head was finally held high as I made my way through the house and to the front door. Nothing could take away my happiness. Not even the demons in Jackson. I had the green light to control them now.

CHAPTER 5

CAMAYA

Bright and early, I had begun my usual routine of making breakfast before my daughter or my man had rose out of bed. I was able to put on my makeup first after showering, and donned my white, silk robe over my bra, bodice, and stockings. That way, after breakfast, all I had to do was put on my clothes and shoes.

When I flipped the last four pancakes, I took down the plates from the cupboards and almost dropped them at the sound of my mother's voice.

"Just look at you," she said from the archway of the dining room.

I turned to the island and held the four plates in my hands. With a somber look on my face, I passed her to get to the dining room table.

"You look like a real mother and wife right now. Got breakfast all made up and you're setting the table. Got yourself put together, so that when your man wakes up, he'll see something beautiful instead of something mutated and disheveled."

"It's the way it's been," I said quietly. Then, I returned to the kitchen for glasses and flutes.

"I underestimated you, Camaya."

"I know."

"Let me help with that." She went to the countertop near the stove and grabbed the last of the glasses and flutes.

I whooshed past her to take out the pancakes and shovel them onto the platter on the other side of the stove.

"You're so coordinated," she commented. "You have it looking and smelling good in here like a real sitcom family."

"Can you open those curtains over that bay window?" I asked her while I grabbed two platters from the island. They were filled with turkey bacon, and quarter sized chicken breast. Then I grabbed the platters that I placed pancakes and eggs on.

My mama followed my lead and picked up the bowls that had oatmeal and mixed fruit in them. "Don't these look scrumptious." She lightly laughed. "Good God, Camaya. No wonder your man is so cut-throat over you. You keep him eating like a king. Girl, you must be one hell of a cook for him to even have moved you all the way out to California."

I fingered my feathery bangs away from my forehead and placed my hand on my hip as I turned to her. "First of all, the house that we own in Calabasas is a joint ownership. I own half of it. Secondly, the only reason that I live in Calabasas is because I worked to get there. It had nothing to do with my food. It was the way I treated him, took care of his home when he was away, and because I loved him like nobody else could."

"I'm just trying to—"

"No, I know what you're trying to do, but you need to understand that I harbor a lot of anger for you over what you did to me. I was a good girl, Mama. I did every-fucking-thing you ever wanted me to do. What did I get in return? You cutting my hair off because you said that I was too vain. You made me wear long skirts and unsightly outfits to keep people from looking at me. Most importantly, you scarred me emotionally. I was so scared and timid, and I couldn't bear to see my own inner-beauty. Had Nas not put up a shit ton of mirrors in the halls and around the first house he had in Calabasas, then I wouldn't have been forced to see who I was for *who* I was. But you know what? I thank you. Because of you keeping me so closed off, I was able to be the perfect, loyal common law wife to a goddamn animal. I was able to maintain a household and accept responsibility for the things that I've done. Because of all the shit you've done, I know how to survive, and I know how to keep a stable home and environment for my daughter. She's the same one that I was carrying when you kicked me out on my ass for being a human."

"Camaya, I'm sorry."

"You can save your sorry. Camaya Webber is good."

"I honestly thought that you would come back home."

"How, Mama? I didn't have no clothes, remember?

You burned them in the parking lot."

"You could've worn something of mine."

"We're not going to walk this road, alright? I got to be Superwoman this morning, because we have a very important memorial to get to. So you're going to have to do what I do, and slap on a mask for my family. They are never to see me weakened, you understand? That means that for the first time in your life, you're going to have to be a mother. A real one. When my daughter sits at this table, you are to greet her, make happy, pleasant conversation, and you will eat whatever it is that I prepared. I booked your flight to California tomorrow, so I don't want to hear anything about how you can't come, Vanessa Webber. Laundry is done on Tuesdays, we eat at seven in the morning, high noon, and seven at night. It's that easy to remember. Even when I'm busy in my office, I'm always on that schedule."

"Your... Your office?"

"I am an elite designer, Mama. I'm in demand like crazy, so you being in California is a win-win for everyone. You can help me with Abby until you decide to move after the deal with Auntie's house is closed."

The sound of an airplane came down the hall, but I knew that it was Nas with Abby. I took a deep breath and raised a brow at her, for her to slap her smile on her face obediently.

"Ladies and gentlemen, we're now landing at the dinner table," Nas said over his invisible intercom. He lowered Abby out of the air and onto her booster seat at the table. Thank God he had put on a shirt before he got her out of bed, or else I would've had to steal him away from breakfast and had him take my girdle off in the bedroom. "Smells good, baby. As always." He leaned over and pecked my cheek. "Morning, Ma Nessa," he greeted her, then took his seat at the head of the table. "*Baby laced me with some turkey bacon,*" he sang into his spoon.

Abby giggled at his side.

I rolled my eyes and pulled out the orange and cranberry juice containers to sit them on the table top.

"*Mommy made me oatmeal!*" Abby sang into her empty plate.

My mama laughed while I took my seat at the other end of the table. "Do y'all always sing at the table?"

"Mommy's food is good," Abby told her. "I like cheese on my eggs."

"Oh, dang," I gasped.

"No, I'll get it," my mama offered. She rose from the table and snagged the block of cheese from the refrigerator, then picked up the last platter off the island that had toast on it. "Camaya, you really did your thing. I have so much to choose from that I'm not sure what I'm going to eat."

"Thank you, Mama," I said lowly. She had never said anything nice to me before. I used to make breakfast for us on Saturday mornings, yet she always scolded me.

"Abby," Nas called her. "This is your grandma. This is your mama's mama."

"I have a grandma?" she asked, shocked.

"You do, baby. You have two of them."

"I *do*?"

"You sure do. You and your mama get to meet your

other grandma today."

"We do?" me and my daughter asked in unison.

"She'll be at the memorial to pay her respects. It's only right."

"Baby, I've never met your mom. I've only heard the horror stories."

"Well, it changes today. I wanted it to be a surprise, but I guess y'all have had enough of surprises."

"Abby," my mama called her with a smile. "Tell me all about you."

"Umm..." she wiggled in her seat for a moment then picked up her fork while Nas scraped a few pieces of fruit onto her plate. "I love Peppa Pig. Oh! I like the color pink. I like to dance, sometimes. I'm four years old, and I can spell really good."

My mama's eyes had become misted. "Y'all she speaks so well."

"That's because Cammy used to read to her when she was in the womb," Nas confessed. "That and the fact that her parents drill her when in public, like have her count stuff in the produce section, or have her recognizing different colors."

"The love in this room is just—" My mama's sentence was cut off due to her choking on her own tears. She saw, firsthand, that the world wasn't as evil as she thought it was. She didn't have to be cruel when she could've had the love and togetherness that Nas and I had provided.

I reached over and grabbed her hand under the table.

"I'm sorry, y'all. I'm just emotional this morning."

"It's cool." Nas chuckled. "Even thugs cry."

"Grandma is a thug?" Abby asked through a gasp.

"No, baby." He laughed. "It's just an expression.

"Oh. Well… thugs cry too, Grandma!"

We all got a good laugh off that and enjoyed breakfast together. There were no more tears. Not until we reached the church that was full to capacity.

We left my mama behind so that she could get herself together. Nas and I had packed the majority of the house, so there wasn't much left to do when we got back except for change clothes, place the ones we had gotten out of in our luggage to pack them, along with our toiletries, strip Abby's bed, and have the movers to come and take all of our furniture to a local Goodwill. It was going to be hard to say goodbye to that house, since it was where I found myself, Nas and I fell in love, and I delved into my talent for the first time. Maybe it was our home, but now someone else would be able to experience the love that those walls had seen.

I guided Nas down the aisle of the church so that we could sit on the first pew with Conz, his date, Meech, and Milla. Puff had so much respect from people in the neighborhood that we had to actually wiggle through a very small place at the doors. We were actually early by twenty minutes, so for the church to be filled to the max only told you what type of man he was.

Meech had his head held high with his shades over his eyes. I couldn't have been the only one to pray that he wouldn't pass out and have another seizure. Jamilla squeezed his hand on his knee, while Conz rubbed his back. Nas seated me and Abby, then sat down next to us.

We were thankful that the others were able to save us a seat. Before the ceremony began, others from around Jackson were able to go up to the black and gold casket to view him one more time, which would explain why they were all here early.

After a while, my man sniffled. I laced our fingers together and squeezed his hand a little tighter. I hated to see all the men so damaged over the loss of Puff, but it only proved that— unlike what Nas had said to me years ago— they could actually feel.

Three hours. From nine to noon, we were there, listening to all of the beautiful memories that people shared of the late man who seemed so full of life.

Row by row, we all got up and viewed Puff one more time. Surprisingly, Meech didn't fall to his knees or fold inside of himself. Conz and Nas embraced him with glistening cheeks. No one was able to show their eyes. My guess was that they were all bloodshot from the silent tears that they shed.

Suddenly, a tall and slim woman walked up to Nas, placing her hand gently against his shoulder. He turned to

93

look at her and immediately grabbed her up inside a tight hug. The two rocked for a while and shared a few words that I couldn't hear with them being at least ten feet away from me. The woman took her black, silk glove across his cheek to rid it of the tears that had fallen over his father-figure. Then she hooked her arm within his and guided him down the aisle.

He sniffled and released her arm when he was close to me. "Baby, I want you to meet Sady. She's my womb donor."

She swatted his arm and threw on a smile for me. "Hello, beautiful! I'm so glad that he didn't choose a ratchet. Praise the Lord! Won't He do it?"

"I guess so." I nervously giggled. "It's nice to meet you."

"Tim, I thought you wanted me to meet your wife *and* daughter? Where is she?"

Nas looked over his shoulder at Abby being passed from Jamilla's hip to Meech's. "With her uncle. I ain't gettin' her back for a while."

"Well, are y'all still coming to the house? I want to see her and spend time with her. You said that we would catch up."

"We will, Sady. I just didn't expect for you to show up and pull me to the side."

"Alright. Well, I guess I'll see y'all when y'all get there. Be prepared to eat too. I've been up all night, cooking. I mean, I wasn't really expecting anybody, but it was a nice gesture so that I could invite some folks."

"Same house?"

"Boy, I know you know where I live. Ain't you the one with goddamn eyes—" She slapped her hand over her mouth and looked around for a second to make sure that no one had noticed that she had cursed inside the church. "Look, you got me cursing in the house of our heavenly Father. Be there in an hour. I'll have everything set up."

He nodded and sent her on her way. Though I threw up a shy wave to salute her, she didn't say anything. Like mother, like son. They both were short on words.

Nas placed both his hands gently at my waist and

pulled me into a gentle kiss. "You ready to go home?"

"Yes," I quietly replied.

"Good. Saying goodbye won't be as hard as I thought it would've been. I'm sorry that I didn't do this a long time ago, Cam. I didn't mean to make you uncomfortable, and I damn sure didn't want you to hate me. Something here was pulling me back in, and I think I figured it out."

"What's that?"

"I had yet to close that chapter with my mama. Today, I get to. In the morning, we can go ahead and get the fuck up out of here with nothing to hold us back." Slowly, he lifted my chin and kissed my lips so passionately that I could've passed out. It had been a while since he had kissed me like that. Why he chose to do it inside a church only baffled me.

"Slow down, heathen," I joked. "Your father figure is over there in a casket, and your mama just walked away. Not only that, but God is watching."

"He's *always* watching." Jokingly, he bit into my neck and leaned away to see the expression on my face.

I was only thankful that he was in a good mood, with his goofy ass.

CHAPTER 6

NAS

Going back to my old house was nothing short of surprising. I left that bitch when I was sixteen and didn't look back. The only thing to change was the furnishings. Other than that, my mama didn't change the wallpaper or the paint of the walls. I led Camaya in by the hand, holding my daughter's small hand in the other. We had changed into white tops and denim bottoms. We all styled the same all-white Retro Jordan 11's. I loved to match my family. We were all unified that way.

When my mama came out of her bedroom, she was wearing a long white tank top and had slipped into a pair of dark blue skinny jeans. She looked like she belonged with the family. She looked down at Abby after she turned the corner from the hallway into the living room.

A smile exploded onto her face as her height decreased with her damn near kneeling to spread her arms at my daughter. "You are just the cutest chubby thing I've ever seen in my life! Come and give your Grammy a hug!"

Abby looked up at me first, then at Camaya. Slowly, she let go of our hands and took her time to walk over to my mama for a hug.

"Oh my goodness, she smells so good, Tim. She's so soft and pretty."

"Alright now, you're treating my kid like she's an orange at the grocery store," I remarked.

She pulled away from Abby and shot daggers at me through her eyes. "Hush. You should be lucky that you made a pretty baby. With the way you used to score on Conz and Meechie, I thought that your kids were gonna come out with some kind of deformity."

"Well, Abigale *Asaad* is perfectly fine."

"Now, hold on, Tim. I'm fine with you changing your name to Nasir and all that, but it's not fair that the baby got to suffer. What's next? You gon' make your woman change her last name to somethin' Arabic too? That name ain't the one that runs through your veins. My daughter-in-law and my grandbaby deserve the name that my daddy gave me. It's the same name I gave you."

"Sady, we ain't gon' argue over this."

Abby gasped and clasped her chubby hands over her mouth. "You called your mommy by her first name."

"Yes, I did."

She looked over at Camaya with her eyes hooded, debating on if she wanted to try it out on her own mother.

"Don't you even think about it." I chuckled. "I will not be held responsible for you being in time-out when you're supposed to be enjoying your grandma, Abby."

"Time-out?" my mama screeched. "Lord, this is what I get for not being the mother that I was supposed to be. You can't just put a child in time-out and expect everything to be alright, *Nasir.*"

"Actually, you can when they're the only child." For some reason, bitterness took over me. I tried to swallow it, but that darkness consumed me.

100

"Don't you put my grandbaby in time-out. You have to take away toys, or—"

"Make them work until they pass out because bills need to be paid?"

Silence fell over the room. I blinked, remembering where I was and who was around me for a second. Never did I want my daughter thinking that I was a bad person. I was, but that wasn't for her to know.

Camaya stepped away to check an alert that popped up on her phone, and that made me feel so lost and shaky. I needed my sweetness at my side to balance me out. If only she knew the type of shit I got into without her, then she would've left my ass a long time ago.

"I didn't mean any harm," my mama said. "I just—"

"No, Ma. I'm sorry for snapping on you."

Her neck bucked back. "Well, that's a first. A kid and a woman did your rude self some good. Had this been six years ago, you would've kept on going without thinking of an apology."

"Yea, well, I have to show my daughter what type of

101

husband she's supposed to have."

"Babe," Camaya sweetly called me. She then handed me her phone and placed her hands inside the back pockets of her jeans. "Don't be mad."

"I'm not," I merely mumbled with my eyes on her screen. It turned out that our flight had gotten delayed and pushed back a day. Instead of choosing to have to reschedule the flight, Camaya had chosen the day after tomorrow to leave. "Abby has bereavement at school, anyway. She'll get a little more acquainted with her grandmothers before we go."

"Go?" my mama asked with disgust. "Where are you going?"

"Back to California."

"So, it was true? You did move all the way out to the west coast?"

"It was what was best for my daughter and my wife. Hell, it was better for me."

"Nas, I just… never mind."

"No," Camaya spoke. "I think it's best that y'all get

whatever off your chests. Especially before we go back home."

"Honey, you got to understand that he is who he is and it's because of me. Ain't no talkin' to him when he gets this way."

"What is it that you would like to see him do?"

"I don't know. Even if I did, I wouldn't want to discuss it in front of the baby."

"How about we all eat, then? Yea. You would like that, wouldn't you, babe?" She rubbed my arm with her infamous smile intact.

"Fine." I didn't want to sit down but coming together as a family was more important than my attitude or the way I felt about my mama at the moment.

My mama and Cam hit it off. Abby enjoyed my mama's greens, even though she couldn't stand eating collards. It didn't matter how many times my mama wiped her face off, it would get messy all over again.

"What are your parents feeding granny's baby?" she

103

asked Abby.

"Some of everything healthy," Cammy giggled.

Suddenly, my mama reached over the table and grabbed my hand. Her eyes were so pure that I could've sworn that someone else's soul had jumped into her body. "I'm sorry, baby," she said sincerely. "Not just for being a bad mother, but for practically taking your youth away. It wasn't my intention. I only hope that one day you can forgive me. I know I was a horrible person, but I can't be here and not be a part of this family. I don't give a damn if I have to apologize every five minutes, Nasir. I will be here. I will call you by your chosen name and I will respect the fact that your wife will one day have the last name you chose for yourself and your daughter. As of now, do we have an agreement before you carry my family back to California?"

My eyes darted over to Camaya. I needed a little bit of my wife's innocence and positivity before I could give an answer. A part of me wanted to tell my mama to go to hell. The other part of me wanted to be an adult and to show my daughter that she couldn't just curse her way out of situations. I had to let go of what I *wanted* to do just to be a husband and father; the head of the family.

Faintly, I nodded. "We have an agreement," I mumbled.

My mama got up from her side of the table, walked around and hugged my neck. "I promise that neither of us will regret this moment." Then she kissed my cheek, which formed an instant smile on my face for someone reason.

After a while, we had gotten stuffed, laughed and talked, and I had even gotten a text from Meech, letting me know that they weren't going to be able to make it. He just wanted to lay up with Milla for a minute before he headed back home. When I looked up at Camaya's face, she wasn't my happy baby. She was looking down at her phone with her lips pressed tightly together.

"Babe?" I softly called her.

Her eyes shot up to me.

"What's wrong?"

"She went back," she said somberly.

"What?"

"Whatever. I tried. I did what any kid would do for their mother. It is it was it is."

"What's the matter with my pretty?" My mama asked as she sat back down in her seat with a cup of coffee in her hand.

"My mama went back to the guy that was abusing her," Camaya explained. "We just took her out of that hell hole last night."

"Baby, some women are just weak minded over men. I wasn't the best to your man, but he can honestly say that he has never seen me chase no damn man. You did all you could do. It was her choice to go back. You can't leave that on your head as your fault."

"But Mama, what if something happens to her?"

"Then you need to remember that it was her decision. Not yours."

Camaya bowed her head. My baby was hurting so badly that I didn't know what to do for her, if anything.

"But... Then again... You can remember that you're a Richmond-Asaad and go to drag her ass by her ankles, put homeboy in his place, and strap her ass down in the seat on the plane to take her to Cali without giving a fuck about her feelings."

My jaw slid open. I had to slam my hand down onto the table top. "I was wondering when the fuck my real mama was gonna show her face. How dare you sit behind whoever the fuck was here before. I was about to say, I know damn well you're not just gonna sit there and pitch that Lollipop Guild bullshit to my woman. You used to bring the noise back in the day."

"I damn sure did." She shrugged as she sipped her coffee. "Now, baby, if you're that worried, you go and get your mama. A mother's love is grand, but a child's love is even grander. Snatch her ass up and throw her over your shoulder."

"Baby!" Camaya squealed with her eyes on me. "Can you hear your mama?"

"She's *your* mother-in-law, and I'm with the shits. I say we go and get *my* mother-in-law and take her with us."

"And if she leaves California in the middle of the night?"

"Don't worry about that part. You know I got eyes. I can put out a word to hit our line if they see her. And if it gets real bad, they can just snatch her, and we'll bring her back."

My mama kissed her teeth. "That's that gangsta shit I'm talkin' about!" She threw her hand up over the table, slapping five with me.

Camaya squeezed her temple. "What the hell am I thinking, to marry into this craziness?"

"Hey, now! From what I can tell, you're the calm to my son's storm. You're the politeness to his rudeness. You're a perfect fit. Hell, I didn't have no perfect fit, so you can imagine how bad I was."

I chuckled at her remark. She was right though. My mama was out of her damn mind back in the day. Camaya just didn't know how worse off I would be without her. Hell, how horrible I would be without her *and* Abby.

CHAPTER 7

NAS

Thank God that Abby was still awake by the time we had gotten back to the house. Camaya looked out of the window as if Laz posted against his car was some kind of illusion.

I looked in the backseat at my daughter and pulled one of her earbuds out. "Baby, you remember your mama's friend? The one who gave you the necklace?"

She nodded.

"Well, I have something to tell you about him."

Camaya's head snapped toward me as if to try and gage what I was doing.

"Baby, some people don't have families, okay? However, some people have more than one mama and more than one daddy. You... You have two daddies. One who helped to make you, and then you have me, who is helping to raise you."

"Two daddies?" she asked with her eyes wide and her little jaw wide open.

"Yes, Abby. Your mama's friend is your other daddy. Would you like to speak to him again?"

She happily nodded.

"Good. He's going to spend some time with you until we go back home, okay?"

"Kay, Daddy."

Camaya placed her hand on top of mine before I got out to open her door. "Thank you, Nas," she said with cloudy eyes.

I responded with a smile, praying at the same time that Abby wouldn't run Laz off with her loads of questions.

After letting Camaya out, I kissed her full on the lips, then unstrapped Abby out of her seat. When we were close enough, I put her on her feet, slapping hands with Laz.

"Are you going to cry again?" Abby innocently asked.

Laz chuckled as he squatted to try and meet her at eye-level. "I might. Crying's not so bad."

"Are you really my other daddy?"

He swallowed hard, but the smile she gave him didn't leave his face. "I am."

"How come I don't know you?"

"That's because I did something very bad when you were in your mama's tummy. Your other daddy had to protect you, because I was a mean, mean person."

"Oh, you got a timeout. I get those too."

All of us had to laugh at her assumption.

I let her hand go and said, "You're going to go and play with Lazarus for a little while, and then we're going to get some sleep before have to go to the airport in the morning. For now, your mama and I are going to go and break down the beds and make sure that everything is packed up already."

"Kay, Daddy."

"Be good, and don't talk Laz's ear off."

"Laz?" she asked with her nose turned up. "What kind of name is Laz?"

"What kind of name is Abby?" he returned.

"It's Hebrew. My name is Abigail. It means *a father's joy.*"

"Oh, really?" He took her by the hand, leading her around the side of the house. "Well, I was named after a really old man in the bible who was risen from the dead."

"Zombie!"

Camaya stuffed her hands inside her back pockets and strolled over to me with a tilted head. When I thought she'd hit me, she only laced her hands around my neck, staring me deeply in the eyes. "We gotta break the beds down, Nas?" she questioned. "And why would we need to do that when we're giving them away to Goodwill?"

I shrugged. "To give Abby some time with her biological father?"

"You sneaky little something or other."

Her belly pressed into mine. That's when I noticed that she wasn't wearing a waist cincher. She was only four months pregnant, but she was barely showing. I could feel how hard her stomach was when she was that close. A feeling of joy overtook me. My life was complete with the family we had, but I knew this shit was far from over. We might be leaving Jackson behind, but the drama would soon unfold. I could feel it. People like me weren't allowed to stay happy for too long.

CAMAYA

Stepping back into my own home in Calabasas almost made me cry. Though I wished I could chuck it up to pregnancy hormones, I couldn't. There was a chance for my mother and I to reconcile. She wanted to, but her own demons had once again pulled her away from her own daughter.

"Mommy," Abby called to me.

I turned my head to see her standing right next to me with her pig clutched at her chest. "Yes, baby?"

"When are we going to see Uncle Meechie and Aunt Milla again? Is Uncle Conz coming to us now?"

I mustered a smile for her. "I'll tell you what. We can call them and get them all to come and visit for a few days. That sound like something you want to do?"

She nodded, just before Nas came up behind her and scooped her off her feet. He carried her into the living room and turned on the TV for her. Two other men had passed me in the foyer with our luggage and a few pieces of art and memorabilia that I didn't want to leave in Jackson this time around. Nas had told me on the plane that he was in negotiation to put the old house up for sale. I wasn't so sure how to feel about it, but I knew that I couldn't always keep everything to myself. The Egyptians had even tried to take their valuables with them to the after-life, and we see that it was an epic fail. So why should I try to hold on to such unimportant things?

Tonight, we ordered takeout, lounged around as a family, then turned it in for the night. As usual, after putting Abby to bed, Nas walked around the house to make sure it was locked tight, and I was fresh, in my teddy, in bed. I couldn't even read, for some reason.

By the time Nas had come to bed, I said the first thing that was on my mind. "I'm going to promote Lucy to VP."

He had paused, midways taking his shirt off. The blank stare he gave me was almost comical.

I shrugged. "I figured since we're going to have a small child and an infant now, that I'm going to finally take Puff's advice about trusting people with my brand. Lucy

115

has no children, so she can do a lot of the traveling. She knows the staff very well. We even have money in the budget to get her an assistant if need be. Maybe even an intern. Most of them work for free anyway, right?"

"Baby, slow down," he said, finally freeing that glorious body of his from his pajama bottoms and t-shirt. "Where's all this coming from?"

"Well, you're going to be home a lot more, and you've made necessary sacrifices for your family. It's not fair if I don't. It doesn't matter if I do the footwork or not at this point. Either way, I'm still paid, just like you. So like you, I'm trusting someone else with the company so I can have more time for my family. I miss you so much when you're away, and sometimes when you're right here. I felt like we were going to end when we were in Jackson, Nas. That's not what I want. This is all I know."

"Camaya, baby, I completely understand you, but you live and breathe your career. I don't think I'm comfortable with this."

"We said that we wouldn't get married until my career died down a little, right? Well, what if it just keeps rising over the next twenty years? We're going to have grown kids and we still won't be legally married. Nas, I'm ready."

"Ready for?"

"I'm ready to give this thing my all. I'm ready to be Mrs. Camaya Asaad, finally."

A smile pulled across his face. "You... You mean that?"

"Yes. You've waited a mighty long time."

Nas pulled the covers back on my side, then gently removed my glasses. Once again, I had forgotten that I was wearing them. His lips softly grazed against mine. "Who knew that with all the bad women I've had in my day, I would be marrying the *fat* girl who wore those long skirts and shirts with sneakers?"

"Shut up." I giggled. "I'm glad my mama burned all of those shits."

"Come here, Mrs. Asaad. I have a premarital present for you."

"Do you, now?"

"Yes, ma'am."

Carefully, I climbed on top of Nas while fusing our lips together.

NAS

"Abby, calm down, baby," I stressed, while pushing the buggy down the aisle inside Trader Joe's. She was going nuts for chocolate chips.

Camaya had gone to the airport to pick up Meech and Milla, and Conz would be an hour and a half behind them. We made Abby's wish come true two months after being back home. The hard part wasn't getting everybody together. It was the fact that I had to pick up last minute items that Camaya had to prepare.

"Daddy, chocolate!" Abby screamed, whacking me with Peppa.

Abruptly, I stopped the cart and looked down at her with a stern eye. I wasn't sure if it was the fact that I wasn't traveling like I normally did that had my nerves on edge, or if it was because I didn't have a means to get away from the everyday noise my daughter created when she was home from school. Whatever the reason, I had the urge to pop her.

Instead, I coldly said, "We act like a lady and a gentleman when in public, do you understand, Abigale? Because girls who don't act like ladies gets a mean timeout without Peppa Pig, and guys who aren't gentlemen end up getting yelled at by their wives. It's in your best interest to act like you have sense in this store before I put you in the corner at home."

"But I want chocolate chips," she whined.

"Daddy said no. That's it. Ask me again, and I'm giving you a timeout. I'm not playin' with you."

Just as I was turning the corner at the end of the aisle, I almost bumped carts with a woman who was wearing a scarf fashionably draped over her hair and a white, silk princess cloak.

"I'm sorry," I apologized.

Before she could speak, her husband stepped around the corner, who was the brother I had seen months ago, who had given me the pamphlet about joining the Nation of Islam. He brought a smile to his face and extended his hand to me.

"We meet again, my brother." He chuckled.

I accepted his hand and simply nodded.

"Must be fate."

"Either that, or we just shop at the same store."

"Have you given any thought—"

"I don't mean to interrupt you, brother, but I really have to get moving."

"No interruption. You should really give it some thought. When you set yourself free... *truly* free... you seek the truth in all things." With a tip of his hat, he grabbed his wife's elbow and continued on as if he had said nothing.

I stood there for a few more minutes, thinking of what he had said. The only thing that I was truly afraid of was losing my family. What truth could there be in that?

After unstrapping Abby and letting her out of the car, I gave her two light bags to carry. No matter how much money she gained in this life, I was teaching her not to be a sorry woman. Her mother wasn't one, so she wouldn't grow to be one either.

Noticing the car on the street in front of my house, I knew that Conz had made it at least. My suspicion was verified when he, along with Meech, came out to help me with the bags, but there wasn't really much to get.

With his t-shirt over his shoulder, Conz twisted his lips up. "You got that, bro. I came out here for nothing."

"What's good?" I chuckled as I closed my trunk.

"Got somebody in the house I want you to meet. It's a surprise for all of y'all. I want organic responses from all of y'all."

"Organic?"

Noticing the look on my face, Meech took a single grocery bag from my left hand while shaking his head. "Her name's Michelle, and you're about to be surprised."

I scrunched my face as I tread to the doors of my home. To my surprise, after falling into the foyer, all I heard was laughing and chatting before I could even see my kitchen.

"Oh, babe!" Camaya exclaimed as she slid off the barstool with a flute in her hand. "Baby, come and meet Michelle!"

"Yea, Nas," Jamilla added as she raised her glass in the air. "I'm still trying to figure out how much money Conz paid her to say that they were together."

Conz bucked at Jamilla when he passed her. The Michelle woman, dressed in a pair of light blue scrubs, stood with a decent smile and extended hand.

"Nice to meet you," I greeted her.

"Nice to meet you, too. You have a very lovely home." She took her fingers through her light brown hair, and I noticed right off that there was no tan from a wedding ring. Plus, her nails were properly groomed and manicured. Through her smile, I could see perfect teeth that were sparkly white.

My stomach knotted. I had to go around the island and

fetch a bottle of wine out of it. Fuck using a glass, I took that shit to the head.

Conz smacked his teeth. "Come on, man. You and Milla are embarrassing me. Why y'all got to do all that drinkin'?"

I swallowed hard, pivoting to catch his line of sight. "She's *normal*," I responded through a heavy breath.

Meech busted out laughing with Abby on his arm. "That's what I said!"

Camaya slapped my arm. "Nas, quit it. Don't you want to know how they met? I mean, it's clear that she didn't fly here from Georgia."

"You live here?" I questioned. Only one of my eyes was squinted. I was trying to get a read or a handle on this woman. She was real. She was standing before us all with not a blemish or a blush. Conz? A real woman?

Michelle giggled as she strolled over to Conz, who was propped against the island. Slowly, she coursed her hands over his shoulders and around his neck. "Would you like to tell them how you had to practically stalk me?"

"Nope, because I already believe you," Jamilla said.

Conz cut his eyes at her.

"Well, I was at a Bronner Brother's event with my sister when I first ran into him." Michelle smiled while recalling the events. "I wasn't one for busy events, but my sister insisted because I was on vacation. I heard this woman yelling about a heart attack, and because no one helped, I used my medical skills to see what all the fuss was about."

"That was my damn mama," Conz grunted. "Every fuckin' weave she saw, she just had to go crazy over 'em. This one here thought that my dramatical ass mama was for real."

"Knowing that there was a possibility that she could've had a real heart attack, I offered to stick by her for the rest of the event."

"I declined."

"By chance, I ran into him at the Waffle House, about three hours later."

"My mama tripped her, and she landed in my lap."

124

"We were embarrassed but we played it off very well."

"So…" Conz wrapped his arms around her waist and looked down into Michelle's light brown eyes. That's when I noticed that he was absolutely smitten by her. He had never looked at any of his other women the way he looked at her, with a light smirk and his head tilted while holding his eye contact with her. "We exchanged IG info, DM'd for a hot little minute, then moved on to Facebook, and finally exchanged numbers when we felt that neither of us was crazy."

"Oh, you hated the fact that I lived in LA."

"Despised that shit with a passion." He chuckled. "I didn't even come to visit my bro because he was out here, and he has my niece."

"That's so gay," Jamilla said. "But you know what, Conz? I'm happy for you. Finally, you don't have a gold-digging, ratchet ass chick that doesn't have your best interest at heart. Oh, *and* she was willing to take an hour trip out of the blue, just because you told her you had a surprise for her, right after she got off work. I love her already. Congratulations."

"Thanks, Milla." He didn't take his eyes off Michelle.

To be honest, neither did I. Even though she appeared to be perfect, I couldn't shake the fact that maybe she had ugly feet or some shit.

CHAPTER 8

CAMAYA

Michelle was like a Godsend to the family. Over the course of two months, we hung out every chance that we got. Whenever Lucy and I would go to get new fabrics in LA, I would call up Michelle for lunch or dinner. She was more into Conz than everyone else thought she was. The only night she was at my home, she helped me and Milla with the dishes, and she was even my workout partner twice a month. I didn't want to gain too much weight during my pregnancy, even though it would be difficult when Coachella arrived because I'd be pregnant in the heat.

Today, I was bent over while taking clothes out of the dryer, and all I heard was, "Good God almighty. Look at this here."

A smile stretched across my face as I stood. There was always something about me wearing tennis shorts and knee-high socks that drove my man up the wall. Swiftly, I turned to see him leaning against the pane of the entryway, shirtless, with his chest and abs glistening. He must've had a good workout in the home gym. For the new baby, he was tightening and toning everything. He said it was to be able to keep up with Abby and the new little one. To me, he was only trying to get raped.

"Can you go and stalk someone else?" I asked politely.

Slowly, with a devious smile, he shook his head. "That baby is doing your body some serious good, Mrs. Asaad."

Playfully, I rolled my eyes and took the basket off of the dryer where I had already put dried clothing in, and took the back set of steps up to our room. After sitting the basket on the bed, I started straightening up our nightstands when I noticed that his phone was still on the charging pad. It was blinking, and the name of the person calling him from Facebook made my nostrils flare. *Doni Too'Fine.* The profile picture was of Donica holding an Ace of Spades bottle in her hand. I let it go after it stopped blinking and had gone to the inboxes. She had called him over a series of days, yet they were all missed calls.

Deciding not to pry and to trust my man, I took his Xbox Live magazines off the nightstand and placed them underneath. There, I found a book that Nas hadn't talked to me about. *The Holy Quran— The English Edition.* I squinted, trying to figure out why he would need one, when it was never discussed with me that he was even thinking of changing religions. Hell, I hadn't known him to have a religion, period, let alone seeking one.

When I stood again, a set of hands curved around my waist, accompanied by thick, soft lips at my neck. That should've calmed me enough when the screen of his phone began to blink again. Donica was calling.

"Why the fuck does this girl persist on calling you, Nas?" I asked him sternly.

He stopped kissing my neck, only for a moment to see that she was.

Before he could grab his phone, I snatched it off the charging pad and answered for him. I didn't say anything. Instead, I pressed the video key so hard that I thought my coffin nail was going to pop off.

She answered without hesitation, yet she didn't look put together at all. Her orange hair was all over her head and there were dark circles around her eyes. She looked like she had been on one hell of a binge, and she had been crying for a while.

"What the fuck?" she asked.

I pivoted to show Nas in the shot. "Why do you keep calling him, Donica? Is there something that *we* can help you with?"

"First off, just because you're pretending to be his wife, it doesn't mean that you are."

"Get to the point of why you're stalking Nasir, because after this call, I'm blocking you from all social media outlets."

"Girl, fuckin' kill yourself. Your whole life is a lie. Tell her, Nas!"

"Yes, please. Tell me, Nas, so I can get her off this line and commence to blocking her so you can come behind me and block any page she tries to contact you on."

He shook his head. "Donica, I wasn't tryin' to talk to you back in Jackson, and I ain't tryin' to talk to you now. Tell me what it is you want so we can get this over with."

"Nigga, I love you!" she shouted at the top of her lungs. It was so loud that the sound cut out for a second. "How're you just gonna parade around here with this fat ass bitch? I gave it to you right! I was there when you had coke binges and when you attempted suicide a few times! It wasn't her! All these motherfuckers lookin' at me like I'm crazy because Jamilla's bitch ass cousin Jalissa posted a video of me snortin', when it's *your* fault! You introduced me to this shit, but then you skip out on me to be with this hoe? She was fuckin' you and Laz at the same time and I got proof!"

"Enlighten us," I said with squinted eyes. "I'll entertain your shenanigans. Show us some kind of proof that I was with Nas and Laz at the same time. See, the problem is that I was with neither of them when I was pregnant with my child, because Laz shunned me, and Nas was getting to know me. That was a three to four-month span. Go ahead and show your proof."

"Ugh! Bitch, fuck you!"

"Animals always lash out when they're cornered and caged. You take care of yourself and stop stalking mine before I send someone to you, Donica." With that, I hung up and went to her profile to block the bitch. She could kiss my entire ass for what she tried to pull.

"Baby," Nas called to me. "I'm sorry about that. That bitch is crazy."

I handed him the phone back with a smile. "You should've blocked her a long time ago, Nasir. Now, explain to me why there is a holy book for Muslims under the nightstand."

He gulped, awkwardly scratching the back of his neck with his free hand. "Just been doin' some reading." Casually, he strolled over to the other side of the bed and took a seat. "I ran into this guy before we went back to Jackson when Puff passed. Then again a month after we had gotten back home. I don't believe in coincidence, and you know that. So I went to a bookstore and found the Holy Quran. It opened my mind to a lot, babe."

"Why wouldn't you tell me that? It seems that every

time we get better, you close off the communication somewhere. I don't like that. Especially when knowing that this hood rat ass bitch has been contacting you."

"Baby, she don't mean shit to me. You know that. I figure that since it was out of sight then it would be out of mind. I didn't lead her on in any way."

"How the hell does she know about your binges and your suicide attempts, Nasir? You didn't even tell *me* that."

He fingered for me to join him on my side of the bed with his head bowed. I did, having him to wrap his arm around my shoulder and pull my head into his chest. For him to have been working out, he still smelled of fresh Axe body spray.

"Camaya, I hit a low. I was making the money and everything that I had wanted in life was coming to fruition. I had women surrounding me, me and my boys were living it up, and it was like the world was at my feet. Still, I was missing something. I didn't know what it was. So I started snortin' for a thrill. Donica was just a chick who was always around the crew. As you know, we passed her ass around. She caught me one day when I was playin' a

133

deadly game of Russian Roulette with some white cats. She tried to convince me that it wasn't the way, but it was just the coke I was on that had me thinkin' I was invisible. I wasn't addicted. I snorted to fill some void, babe. One day, after doin' her, I got a bad batch of that shit, and I guess it made me start talkin' crazy. All I remember was standin' in the bathroom with a razor at my wrist. The last time I was leavin' a club, she jumped her ass in the car, and I started speedin' down the wrong side of the street. I'll never forget how she screamed and begged me to stop, just like I won't forget how I told myself that I didn't have shit to live for. A few weeks later, Puff let us know that he had connects for us in separate parts of the country. I thought that was the answer to what I was seeking. But then, you came along. That's it."

I looked up at him and kissed his cheek. "Was that so hard for you?"

"Yeah." He chuckled. "I didn't want you to know shit like that about me."

"Thank you for opening up to me, baby. I know it was hard, but you want to know something? We're not all so

134

crystal clean."

"What do you mean?"

"The love I didn't get from my mama, I thought I could get that from Laz. It was the only reason that when I opposed in the backseat our first time, and he kept forcing the issue, I surrendered. I figured that if I just stopped fighting and gave him what he wanted, he would give me something in return. In a way, he did. He gave me Abby. All that love my mama didn't give me, I get it ten-fold from my own daughter. The good girl in me that Laz didn't appreciate, you do. Your journey led you to me. And now... we have each other. We even have the family that we both wanted."

Tenderly, he placed his hand over my protruding belly. "You're right. Now, give me the rest of the day to catch up on your chores. I want you off your feet. You're already six months. Really soon, we're going to see our new nugget, and by no means do I want them to come out all disfigured because you don't know how to sit down."

"Shut up." I giggled.

My cellphone rang inside my back pocket. I stood to

answer, finding that it was my mother in law. "Hey, Ma Sady," I greeted her.

"Hey, baby. I think you should sit down."

"Okay." Cautiously, I sat, wondering what the forewarning was about.

"Are you sitting?"

"Yes, ma'am."

"Baby, I told you that I would keep an eye on your mama for you, remember?"

"Yes."

"Baby... her house is boarded up."

"What?"

"Caution tape was over the door and windows. I went asking questions, and there were too many rumors. I checked for her at the hospitals and morgues. I found her, Cammy."

"And?"

"She's unclaimed at the Jackson Memorial Morgue."

My phone dropped from my fingers. A knot strongly

136

formed inside of my stomach that made me double over. Shit, I didn't even know that I was screaming until Nas came rushing up the stairs and barreled inside of the bedroom. He was kneeling in front of me, trying to get me to say something, but I couldn't. My mama always said that there would be no peace when the sirens call. I was one hell of a siren in that moment. So much so, that there was a strong ringing in my ears.

Nas saw the phone on the floor and picked it up. The only thing I could hear him say was, "Ma, go and claim her. I'll have her flown here for a burial. Find out how she died."

I crawled up to the head of the bed with so much on my mind that I would split in half. If only she would've come home with me and Nas, none of this would've happened. She had her faults, but I tried to give her another chance. Then there was the thought of our last few words to one another. I was so nasty to her, trying to make myself feel better.

Fact of the matter is, nobody knows how much more time we have on this earth. It's best that we treat every moment like it's our last, because our clocks would tick up to that doom's day twelve at any given moment.

CHAPTER 9

NAS

Deactivating all of my social media accounts was the best decision that I could ever make, simply because I didn't have to be worried with Donica. My mama still had people lookin' out for her in Jackson. Just thinking of the name of the city made me nauseous. My baby's mama didn't make it out in time, and it took her three or four months to succumb to the curse that it had on everybody.

Today, we were supposed to be catching up with reading to the new baby, but unfortunately, my old crew had to dress in black again, and come together for yet another home going. I found Camaya's mama a nice little plot where she would be buried on a hill. We drove past it every time we went into town, so Cam could see her whenever we drove.

Michelle and Conz made it over first, this morning. Then, Meech and Milla arrived. Judging by the large overcoat she was wearing, I would say that she had something she wanted to tell us, but knowing her, her focus was on Camaya's mental well-being. Finally, Laz rang the doorbell with his shades donning his face.

I slapped five with him and invited him in.

"She alright?" he asked me, looking truly out of place. He was wearing a white polo and white shorts with a pair of icy kicks to match.

"Nah," I lowly responded.

My mama came down the steps with Abby's hand within hers. Even my daughter was dressed in all white. He was taking her to see Aladdin the musical on Broadway in L.A., then take her to Disneyland. I figured he could get out of Jackson for a breather, like my mama, and he could distract Abby from Camaya's pain on this day.

Laz picked her up and propped her on his arm with a smile that matched mine.

"Bye, Daddy," she said to me, then leaned over to kiss

my cheek.

"Be good, Abby. I'm serious."

"Okay." She wildly waved at her aunts and uncles behind me.

Laz dapped me up before taking her out of the door.

I could hear the flick of a lighter behind me, then looked up to see my mama still there, lighting a cigarette on the stairs. She inhaled the smoke and blew it into the air. "I don't give a damn if you hear screaming. Don't none of y'all dart these steps, ya hear? I'll bring Camaya down these stairs. Only come up if I call for you. Everybody understand that?"

"Yea, Ma," I responded just below everyone else.

Soon after she had gone back up the steps, the first thing I heard was my woman scream for dear life. Meech came over to me, wrapping his arm around my shoulder. He must've felt how bad I wanted to go up the steps and tell my mama to leave the drapes drawn, and to leave Camaya be. Truth was that for the last two weeks, Camaya didn't eat like she was supposed to. She barely slept. All she did was cry. My mama and I may have our differences, but I would be torn if she was the one laying in a casket instead of Ma Nessa.

"Milla!" my mama screamed. It made us all flinch. "Chelle! Get up here!"

If only I could dart the steps, I would have. Camaya needed me. I hoped that she'd seen how much I was really trying when she was rejecting me.

CAMAYA

"No!" I screamed at Ma Sady, with my pillow hugged tight against my chest while she dragged me into the master bath. "I'm not going! I'm not going! I'm not *going!*"

"You're getting your ass in this tub, Camaya Webber," she said sternly.

Before I could get off the floor and make a run for the room to lock her inside the bathroom, Jamilla and Michelle appeared in the doorway. Slowly, I backed away with my pillow stretched out in front of me as though it was a weapon.

"Stay away from me," I warned them. "I'm not going down there, and none of you can make me."

Ma Sady lifted my long shirt from behind. When I whirled away from her, Jamilla ripped the shirt from the bottom, Ma Sady snatched my pillow, and Michelle rushed into the shower to turn it on. As if I had been defiled, they pushed me into the shower that I once loved. I had gone horse from all the screaming I had been doing.

It was the only thing to allow me to hear Ma Sady when she said, "Thank you girls. Wait in the room. We'll be out shortly."

"I'll get the flat irons," Jamilla responded.

Suddenly, Ma Sady pulled open the stain glass door with a washcloth gloved over her hand, and her cigarette propped between her lips. "You can fight me all you want, but I ain't gonna let you rob yourself of the chance to say your goodbyes to your mama."

She didn't give me a chance to fight. She instantly scrubbed me. She even lifted my arms up to wash underneath my arms too. I couldn't even feel violated. All I could do was sob and stand there, all until she handed me the soapy cloth to wash my business that she couldn't get to.

Afterward, she stood by while I tightened my robe and brushed my teeth. Jamilla quickly blow dried my hair and flat-ironed it in ringlets. I chose not to wear makeup on this day, simply because I wanted to be the daughter my mama remembered without a painted face.

With slow and heavy steps, I descended the stairs, wearing my baby doll flats, a pair of black slacks, and a blouse I had made months ago in case I had gotten to be as big as I was. I loved the ruffles on the chest of the silk, gold fabric, but today, I couldn't even enjoy it.

Nas caught me in his arms as soon as my foot landed on the base. He squeezed me and almost messed up my hair with how roughly he grabbed the back of my head to keep me in place. "It's alright, baby," he whispered. He was choking up.

"She's gone," I hoarsely cried. "Baby, she's gone."

"I know."

"I don't want to go, Nas. Please, don't make me go."

He pulled back and lifted my chin so I could look into his soft orbs. "If you don't go, you'll do the same thing she did to you. She turned her back on you and abandoned you. You don't want that for her, do you?"

I dropped my head, focusing on his black leather slippers with gold tips on the toes.

"I promise, Cam. Somehow, I'm going to make this up

145

to you if you go. Now, the whole family has gathered in one place. This is all for Ma Nessa. We got to go, baby."

"Where's Abby?" I sniffled, wiping my tears away.

"Baby, I told you that Laz agreed to come and take her for the day."

I looked around the foyer at all the faces staring back at me. How could I have forgotten that her sperm donor would be coming to get her? Was I that lost and so off-track to where I didn't know anything about my daughter? Even after me trying my best to never forget about her, how I felt my mama did me?

Nas laced his fingers within mine to help me out of the door. Saying that it would be easy was actually easier said than done.

During the ride, just a few minutes away from the house, it was deathly quiet. I kept looking in the rearview mirror to check on Abby, but I had to remember that she wasn't there. I felt so heavy, so empty, and even the subtle kicks that the baby made wouldn't move me.

Nas helped me out of the car and to the open space in

the earth, where a lone preacher stood there, waiting for us.

Over the course of his sermon, I couldn't do anything but think. Think of the happy times I had with my mama. And when going back to those moments, I realized that there were none. Then I wondered if I had done something wrong. Something that wouldn't allow her to love me or look at me like I was her daughter. What did I do to where she couldn't be on my side? I would never treat Abby or my unborn the way she treated me.

I laid my hand over my stomach and looked down at how big I had gotten. Nas and I told our doctor that we wanted our baby's sex to be a surprise. She wouldn't tell us what we were having just yet, and I liked it like that. No matter what gender came out of me, I would love it just like I loved Abby. I squeezed Nas's hand with my free hand, taking my eyes to the casket as it was lowered into the ground. I would never be what she was, and that included robbing my children a chance of peace and to save me from harm. I would never want Abby and her brother or sister to stand and cry because of a stupid decision that I made myself. They wouldn't have to question what they did wrong or right, and they wouldn't have to bury me with guilt on their hearts.

"Bye, Mama," I mumbled, accepting a rose from Nas's other hand so I could toss it onto the casket after it stopped six feet underneath our feet.

Nas kissed my cheek and whispered, "I'm proud of you, Cam. You're one strong woman. I know you feel weak right now, but baby, you've taken a lot of pain in stride. I love you, baby. Your mama's in a better place than either of us could give her."

I lightly smiled at him as my throat closed. Another round of tears was threatening to spill over, but not from hurt. It was because I realized that had it not been for her, I wouldn't be so good at being a wife, a mother, and a damn good friend to those who were at the graveyard with us. I learned from her mistakes and sent her home in peace.

————————

I swiped my nose when Nas reached for the doorknob to our home. We heard Ma Sady holler, "Take your goddamn shoes off before you step foot in that foyer! I didn't mop while y'all were gone, just so you can track shit

148

on my floor!"

I cracked a smile, finally, just as a whiff of pine cones stung my nostrils. It proved that you can take the people out of Jackson, but you can't take the Jackson out of them.

"Come on, now. I didn't do all this cookin', startin' earlier this morning, for y'all to slowly come through the door. Let's go. Everybody get a plate. If it's somethin' on there that you don't like, just leave it."

"Your mama ain't changed at all," Conz commented behind us.

"What, boy?"

"Nothin', Ma Sady! What you cook, though?"

"Meatloaf, greens, cornbread muffins, corn, Mac-N-Cheese, sweet potato pies, strawberry cake, fried chicken, potato salad, and I got some ribs out there on the patio in the smoker."

"Damn, Ma Sady," Meech moaned. "You hooked it up, didn't you?"

"Yea, well…" She appeared at the side of the couch where Nas was seating me. "My daughter-in-law is

149

pregnant, ready to pop, and I didn't want her to have to cook for a few days." Quickly, she opened and closed her palm a few times, signaling for me to give her my purse.

Nas, as he had done when I had a long day in heels, had slipped my shoes off my feet and dragged the ottoman under my legs. "I got your food for you, baby."

"Milla, how far along are you?" Ma Sady asked.

Everybody's heads went over to her. She was frozen in place while trying to sit on the far end of the sectional.

"Don't bullshit Mama, now. I knew you before your bee stings were titties. Gone 'head and tell me."

"Ma Sady, today is about Cammy—"

"And she deserves to know when you're giving her, her first niece or nephew by you. So? When are you?"

Jamilla cleared her throat as she stood to remove her overcoat. "Well… uh… Meechie and I are due in five months."

"Five? Girl, stop lying. You look like you're due in three."

"I've packed on weight. What do you want me to say?"

"You better be careful." I giggled. "Nas couldn't keep his hands to himself before this baby, and during both pregnancies, it's like it made it worse."

"Michael!" Ma Sady called for him. Her eyes were on the floor. "Get your ass out of my pots! Don't you forget that I knew you back when you were so scared to kiss Milla that you bit her damn lip."

"Ha!" Conz busted out laughing. "Y'all remember that?" he asked Nas and Jamilla. "Y'all remember when Meech was Brace Face for three years!"

Nas slapped hands with him, pulling him inside a manly embrace where they had to separate, point, and laugh at Meech.

"It's wasn't that he bit her lip one time," Nas laughed. "Milla's tongue ring got caught on his retainer! Remember? He used to wear a retainer for the top row!"

"Brace facin' ass nigga!"

"Y'all better leave my man alone," Jamilla said, working her neck at the two, who were standing directly in

151

front of the TV.

"Or what?" Conz challenged.

"Oh, okay. What about the time you wore your Spiderman undies to the pool, under your swim trunks?"

"Say, man! Nobody would've known what I had on under there, had your ass not gone under water and pulled 'em off of me!"

"Boy, you were seventeen!"

"So? What about the time you kept your perm in too long and it took your edges out? You were walkin' around the hood lookin' like a burned ass Barbie with that plastic ass blond wig."

"Baby! You better get him! Now he's gettin' personal, and I will bust Conz in his mouth!"

"Hey," Nas said calmly. "I think everybody needs to calm down just a little bit. Today, my baby laid her mama to rest—"

"*Hell* nah!" Conz bellowed, tossing his head back.

"Get 'eem!" Jamilla urged him.

Conz undid his cufflinks. All I could do was shake my head because this was the grand stage for the goofiest of them to do what he did best. When I focused on Conz again, he had successfully unbuttoned his black dress shirt, and was squatted with one leg extended, looking at Nas with this unreadable smirk on his face.

"Don't do it, Conz," Nas warned him, looking off at the side of him. "I'm telling you not to do it, bro. You're in my house. Anything could happen to you."

With a cool tone, still crouched, Conz said, "Remember when Nas had twists?"

"Oooh!" everybody, except for me and Michelle, erupted.

"Dead ass maggots on the head, lookin' ass nigga. Them, *'Creeeepy Crawlers'* ass twists."

"Leave my baby's twists alone," Ma Sady warned him through a laugh.

"Then… Nas was Big Worm without the perm, ass."

I had to hold my stomach and double over at that one. He had said it with so much enthusiasm to where all Nas could do was purse his lips and nod silently.

He held his hand up and said, "But y'all do remember when Conz was, *'The only time I buy Rillos is when another nigga rolling'*, ass nigga."

"Boy, if you don't get your gold and black, Marty the Zebra, lookin' ass."

"Fuck you." Nas laughed, kicking at Conz who had yet to stand.

"Y'all are too much for me." Ma Sady giggled. "Meechie, help me make plates. You already have green juice on your shirt."

Meech looked down at his black dress shirt that had two large white strips at the close.

"With your guilty ass. Ain't shit on your shirt. Come on."

Nas's phone rang for the first time all day. He reached inside his front pocket and pulled it out. "Yo! Y'all! Bet money that Laz lost Abby!"

"Nas!" I shrieked. "Don't bet money on that."

"I bet everybody a bill that he's at his rental and can't find her." Nas answered, placing his phone on speaker. "What's good, lil' homie?"

"Hey, umm… hypothetically speaking… and this is *hypothetically*. If I was playing Hide-N-Seek with Abby—"

"Kid, I should've warned you. Don't ever play that game with her. She is the master of climbing into tight spaces. Go to your kitchen and look inside the cabinet that's closest to the refrigerator. She's in there. It's her favorite hiding place."

The line went quiet for a moment, then we all could hear Abby's small voice. "You cheated, Lazarus! You called my daddy! You have to count again!"

"Thank God," he sighed. "I owe you, man. I was about to call the cops. Now, if you excuse me, we still have three hours before the show, and I have to gear up for Disneyland's fireworks show tonight. This little girl is about to break me in half. I don't know how you do it."

"Yeah, well, when you spend enough time with her, you'll get used to it."

"Hopefully—"

"Lazarus!" Abby whined for him.

"Uhh… I gotta go. Everything's good with Camaya, right?"

"She's straight." Nas chuckled. "You just make sure you don't pull your hair out with Abby."

"See y'all later tonight, then."

"Thank you, baby," I said to him, just as he was shoving his phone back inside his pocket.

"For?" He took a seat next to me, wrapping his arm around my shoulders.

"You know… letting Laz in like you're doing. It really means a lot to me."

"I did it for her, babe. I mean, who knows what health risks she might have in the future, yet neither of us will be able to help her. I climbed off my high horse months ago. Abby knows who her daddy is. It's like you said, it's only right for her to know both of them."

"I love it when you tell me that I'm right." I giggled.

"On another note, when the hell did Mama get out here?"

"Sady? She got here about a week ago. She's been keeping us apart from you since she thought you needed some space. I'm glad she brought you out of your trance today."

Suddenly, my entire mood shifted. The thought of my mama never being able to walk this earth again had put a pang in my heart. Nas's soft kiss on my cheek kind of made me feel better, but it was just one of those things that would have to pass.

"Laz isn't leaving L.A. until Monday. You think he'll be able to handle Abby tomorrow too?"

"No." I laughed. "Babe, he's new to this. Abby's going to drive him up the wall."

"Food!" Ma Sady yelled. She swayed around my side of the couch and handed me a plate full of veggies, then gave her son one that had hearty helpings on it.

Meech came right after her with a plate in each hand, giving them to Michelle and Jamilla.

"Where mine?" Conz asked confusingly.

"Right here," Ma Sady said as she handed him his specially made dish.

His eyes lit up at his pile of corn bread muffins and green beans. "You do still know me, Ma Sady," he sang.

It was times like these that I cherished having a real family surrounding me. What I lost, they replaced.

CHAPTER 10

NAS

At 5AM, I was up, doing fifty sit-ups, getting ready to go for a run. My mind was running ramped. I was cool with Laz being with Abby, but I was still a paranoid father. I couldn't dodge certain questions like if he had left a nightlight on for her. If he had made sure she was properly bathed or went to bed on time. I wanted to just stay on FaceTime for the rest of the day after I put Camaya to sleep around three, long after we buried her mother, but I wanted to at least show the dude that he was able to spend time with his seed without me breathing over his damn shoulder. Changing was not my thing. I didn't like change. For Camaya, I was willing to make that exception.

Returning at the house, at close to 8AM, my woman, who was supposed to be in bed, was waltzing around the kitchen with the music on. I pulled out my earbuds as I approached the island.

She gasped and flinched when she noticed me. "Baby." She giggled, running her fingertips over her silk scarf. "Say something when you come in the house."

I grabbed her phone off the island and shut off her music, where she had it blasting through the surround sound speakers using the Bluetooth setting. "Aren't you supposed to be in bed?" I asked her seriously.

"Well... yea, but—"

"Do you want my mama to come down those stairs, and—"

"What in God's name?" she asked. It was too damn late. My mama had taken the back steps, closing her long, silk robe at the chest. "What do you think you're doing, Camaya?" My mama gave her a stern eye and a raised brow.

Camaya looked over at me with a look of shame, to which I threw my hands up. I wasn't in that brawl.

"You are out of your damn mind. Down here, shaking up my grandbaby like you don't have any sense. And look at your feet!"

I leaned over the island to finally notice how swollen her feet were in her knee-high socks.

"Girl, I'm gonna give you five minutes to get up those stairs and sit in the recliner near the terrace doors. That's what your mother-in-law is here for. To take care of the family. And Nasir!"

My head snapped over to her, wondering what the hell she could've been yelling at me for.

"Put your damn shirt on before you get pneumonia in the ass."

"Mama—"

"Put your damn shirt on," she repeated through grinding teeth. "Ain't that how you got this one in the oven. Just walkin' around here naked."

"I went for a run, though."

"Oh, so you're exposing my Camaya's man meat to the world?"

"It got hot, so I—"

"Put your damn shirt on!" With emphasis, she flapped the back of her robe as she made her way to the refrigerator.

I decided to help my woman up the stairs and to the bedroom before either of us would suffer the wrath of my mama's yelling some more.

Moments later, the doorbell ringing was what brought me down the first set of stairs in my jeans and muscle shirt before I could finish dressing for the day.

With Abby on his shoulder, Laz handed my baby girl to me. She was tuckered out, obviously.

"Nas, she wouldn't go to bed," he confessed. "I guess it was the ice cream I gave her."

I ran my hand down my face. "I specifically told you not to give her sweets after five."

"I know, bruh, but if you would've seen the face she gave me."

"I've seen that face you're talking about on more than one occasion. I'm telling you that you'd get used to it."

"That's somethin' else I was meaning to talk to you

about. You want to put her up and step outside with me?"

I nodded and took my baby to her room, slipped her footies off her, and jetted back down the steps. Laz leaned against his rental SUV, puffing a Newport.

"She got to you that bad?" I laughed.

He slowly shook his head with his eyes on the pavement.

"What's up? Spit it out."

"Nas, I don't want to disappoint her, you know? I mean, thank you for letting me be a part of her life, but with me all the way in Mississippi, and her being out here... what if work gets in the way? What if I fuck around and go to prison, missing the rest of her days?"

"You can't think that way. I told you before that, that little girl changed everything about me. I had an idea of all the shit that I wanted for her in life, and what I would be like. As soon as Cam started pushing... everything changed. You got to stay alive and safe, if not for anything or anybody else, you got to do it for her."

He blew smoke from his mouth with his eyes on my

freshly groomed lawn. "I ain't been shit, man. I even once claimed that she wasn't mine. I just don't want to fuck up. You should've seen how I was looking at her while we were at that musical, and at Disney[and. I was just watching and waiting, anticipating her to say something about what she didn't like. She didn't though. I was so nervous."

"You thinkin' about shyin' away from my Abigale?" I squinted at him, trying to figure out what his point was.

"No. I'm saying that I don't want her to constantly travel, and I don't want her to ever have to throw a tantrum when it comes to me. I'm sayin' that I'm thinking of moving here in a few years, just so I can be at her every beck and call. Only, I don't want to fuck up."

I slapped his shoulder and took his cigarette for a puff. "You won't. You got to trust yourself. If you could do so much when Meech had faith in you, especially with how much pressure I put on you, I know that you can make Abby happy."

"Shit, I'm just glad that we're not two bickerin' niggas over an ex and a baby."

164

"Now, that's what you need to focus on."

"Speakin' of which. I have an idea I wanted to run by you, when it comes to Camaya."

"What's that?" I lifted my left brow. Yea, things were cool between us, but who the fuck was he to give me an idea about my wife?

By the time he was done explaining, it all made sense, and it had even made *me* smile. Turned out, dude was sharper than I thought. Camaya was going to be one grinning somebody, after all she had to put up with from me.

CHAPTER 11

CAMAYA

With Ma Sady around, things were fairly easy. The bigger I had gotten; the more responsibility Lucy took on with my business. She would only contact me once a week to give me an update. Everyone pulled their weight to take as much stress off me as possible. I couldn't help but to think of how things were different with Abby. That difference was that Nas was so menacing to others who were near me, and he pushed me through everything I needed to get done before she was born. Now, he was softly spoken, didn't force me to stay in bed, or to keep focused on something. That's because there were two of him under one roof. If Ma Sady felt like I was doing too much, she wouldn't have an issue with snapping her fingers or giving me the same stern eye that her son did.

It had been so long without me being able to cook in

my own kitchen that I felt it might have been changed, and I wouldn't know it. The furthest I could go was the home gym to get on the treadmill for a good thirty minutes. Any longer than that, and Ma Sady would hit the intercom button to tell me to stop shaking up her grandbaby. Food? I was still eating organically, but a lot more. Ma Sady told me that I was trying to starve her grandchild. If I wasn't mistaken, even Abby had started to gain weight. Ma Sady was old school. Childhood obesity was non-existent. A chubby kid to most southerners meant that you were doing your job as a parent or grandparent.

And Nas? Hanging out late, taking late calls, being late to dinner, or having to be called more than twice to come down to eat was a big no-no for Ma Sady. She ran my house with an iron fist. I should've complained, but I didn't. Honestly, there were no complaints. It was clear that she was trying to redeem herself as a parent. She was doing a damn good job.

On this particular morning, I was sleeping peacefully, when I felt I had been sleeping too long. The desolate sound of strings woke me. I was afraid to move because the classical strings seemed to be very close. I found a little strength to turn over, finding Jamilla standing at the foot of my bed, dressed in a pair of sweatpants and a tight undershirt that showed her bulge. On her head, she was wearing a bonnet. For it to be eight in the morning, her face was beat for the gods. Just beyond her were six old white men in tuxedos. Two were playing the violin, two more were on violas, and the last two were playing the bass.

"Milla?" I nervously asked. "Who're these white people in my house?"

She gave me a beautiful smile with tears welling in her eyes. "You have to get up so you can shower, Cam."

"And? That doesn't explain who these people are."

"Come on." She swiped a tear away as she traveled over to my side of the bed.

Uneasily, I moved the covers back and swung my feet over the edge. She led me into my bathroom, turned the shower on, and waited patiently for me to get out. By the time I was done, Jamilla had left a pair of white, silk underwear on the counter for me, and had a white, silk robe hanging up on the bathroom door. I slipped into them,

168

washed my face, and brushed my teeth.

On cue, Jamilla knocked and entered with her bag at her side.

"What's this?" I laughed.

"Remember this is how we first met." She pulled the chair out in front of my vanity for me to sit.

"Hola!" Michelle cheered. Even she was wearing a bonnet, and her makeup was done to perfection.

I turned before I sat to see her and gave her a hug and a smile. "What are you doing here?"

"I'm here to listen to a few funny stories, and to do your makeup when Milla is done with your hair."

"What's going on, y'all? Where is my family?"

"Your birthday is tomorrow, Camaya. We're going to have Camaya Day, today."

I looked at Michelle skeptically, dressed in her cut up jeans, tank top, and shades. "Camaya Day, huh?"

"Yes," Jamilla answered behind me. That quickly, she had plugged up all of her equipment so she could start on my hair. "We're going to give you a sew-in today. Give you something different."

"Milla," I gasped. "I hadn't had long hair in forever."

"I know. Isn't it exciting?"

I playfully rolled my eyes and leaned back in my chair.

Michelle got an earful about how the guys were truly brothers, only with different parents. I even let her know how much she really fit in with me and Jamilla because we were all different. Michelle had many times when she would toss her head back and laugh. There were even a few where she laughed so hard that she cried. Especially about Conz's comebacks for everything. Still, I wanted to know what was going on.

Milla turned my chair away from the mirror while she styled my hair. The suspense was killing me. Then the doorbell sounded.

Michelle got up from a chair that she had dragged in from the bedroom. "I got that." Out of her purse, she pulled a gold, silk ribbon and handed it to Jamilla. "It's time."

"Roger that." She laughed.

I looked up at Jamilla with an uneasy smile on my face. "It's time for what?"

She didn't say a word to me. She slipped the ribbon over my eyes and finished pinning my hair up. Afterward, she had me to stand and remove my robe. I wasn't at all self-conscious to be seen in my underwear. All I heard was that I had to step inside what felt like fabric. The two zipped up what felt like a dress that fit me perfectly, then I was instructed to step inside a pair of flats.

Carefully, they helped me down the stairs, out of the house, and into a car.

"Are y'all going to tell me now?" I giggled.

"Nope!" they answered in unison.

"I swear to God that if this is a photoshoot, I'm going to personally unfriend the both of you on Facebook and unfollow you on Instagram."

Moments later, we came to a stop. One of the women helped me out but prompted me to step carefully. In the distance, I could hear strings again. I blushed because I knew now that this was no photo shoot. I was scared to call anyone's name, so I placed my hand on whoever's shoulder that was in front of me and was careful with my steps. Slowly, the ribbon was untied and slipped from eyes.

I gasped when I saw my man standing before me in a white, velvet sport coat that had soft gold lapels on them. He wore a soft gold bowtie and white dress shirt that brought a glow to his already handsome face. Nas had a freshly trimmed mustache and low-cut beard.

Those supple lips stretched into a smile. "Can you see me, baby?" He chuckled.

Tears cascaded down my face. Thank God I slept in my contact lenses because no one even thought to grab my glasses or ask me if I was wearing my contacts. I could remember the first time I put on a pair of glasses and got a good look at his features. He had the same curly hair that looked wet to the touch, the V-shape but upturned nose, and the flex in his chiseled face when he ground his teeth.

"Shall we?" He curved his arm so I could slip mine inside the opening.

We turned to a preacher who was already waiting for us. I stole glances while the man of God had given us a speech. Conz and Meech were wearing the same velvet, white sport coat, but without the gold of the lapels. Instead, they had gold roses for boutonnieres. At my side was Jamilla and Michelle. Their dresses featured a lace bodice, an illusion neckline, a ribbon-defined waist, and a fluid mesh skirt with a slit on the side. The color of their dresses was the same soft gold. Behind our preacher was a wall of white, yellow, off-white, and soft gold roses. I couldn't help but to smile and cry all at the same time. The only bad part about it was that I couldn't see myself.

When I looked down, I noticed that my dress was similar to the girls', but I had quarter-length sleeves, and my lace wasn't just covering the sweetheart neckline of my dress, it actually met the ribbon around my belly, where it stopped.

"Nasir," the pastor called him. "Do you take this woman to love, honor, cherish, and respect—"

"Wait," I interrupted him. "Babe, we need a license for this."

He lifted his hand over his shoulder, where Meech presented a folded piece of paper. He opened it and handed it to me. "I knew you were too busy to look at what you were signing."

I scanned the page, noticing that my signature was dead on. The only time I remembered signing anything when Nas asked me to, I was watching the Real Housewives of Atlanta, and I was eating my Three Twins Triple Vanilla Bean Ice Cream. I rolled my eyes when thinking of it. He was slick as hell for that one.

"Told the clerk you were on bedrest and flirted with her a little bit. I needed to, in order to pull this off."

Playfully, I slapped his arm with the papers.

"May I continue?" the pastor asked me.

"Yes. Please forgive me."

"As I was saying. Nasir, do you take this woman to be your lawfully wedded wife? To love, cherish, and honor her, until you both part from this earth?"

With a grin, Nas said, "I do."

"And, Camaya, do you?"

"I do," I sighed. This man never ceased to amaze me.

"May we have the rings, please?"

I looked at Jamilla who had given me a ring that I had only planned to buy Nas. I wondered how far back in our DM's she had to go, just to find the picture that I had sent over two years prior. Together, we positioned our rings at the bases of one another's fingers. I couldn't hear anything the pastor was saying, but I agreed to it all. I was busy inside of my own thoughts.

I had come far from being the scared, sheltered little girl that he and everyone else had gotten accustomed to knowing. Nas wasn't even the hellish heathen that he was when we had first met. I thought of how, if I had never gone to look for Laz that day my mama had put me out, how everything would've literally been completely different. Who knows where I would've been, but it wouldn't be in a secluded part of the gardens, with our closest friends and favorite co-workers and employees watching on with tears in their eyes. I wondered if Nas thought the same. Apparently, he didn't regret anything with the way tears were welling in his eyes before he kissed my ring finger.

The pastor lifted his arms to the twenty-something odd people in attendance. "I now give to you, Mr. and Mrs. Nasir and Camaya Asaad."

The gatherers clapped and cheered for us while we saluted one another. Nas's kisses had never felt sincerer, more beautiful, more promising. Carefully, he walked me down the slim path where the staff had laid white carpeting for us. It led all the way to a black Rolls Royce, where Nas pulled the keys out of his pocket and opened the passenger side door for me. I slid in, waiting for him to get in on the driver's side.

"Baby, we have much, much more to see and do today," he said as he closed the door. "If you're mad at this surprise… you're going to be mad at the fact that this is your push present."

"My what?" I screeched.

With a smile, he started the car and pulled away from the gardens.

CHAPTER 12

NAS

To see Camaya so happy, and to have some of the guys from Jackson, who I hadn't caught up with since Puff's memorial all in one place, I was so complete. My first dance wasn't with my mama. It was with my daughter. We took our shoes off and twirled around the floor at Chain of Events so peacefully and gracefully that it brought tears to my eyes. I thought of how I begged and pleaded to keep her. Though she knew now that Laz was also her father, my baby didn't treat me any differently. I was still her Superman, and she didn't dare to call me by my name. Then I thought of how one day, I would be dancing with her on her special day to some guy I was bound to rough up and give a hard time to when she would introduce us.

I smothered my daughter's cheeks with sloppy kisses, handing her off to her uncle Meech so I could have a dance with old, sweet Sady. My mama had already taken off her heels, so I took off my jacket, handing it to Conz, and two-stepped with the woman I could've sworn that I was going to hate for the rest of my life. *Love's Holiday* by Earth, Wind, and Fire was being played as I had suggested to the DJ when we were putting together a stellar playlist a few nights ago. I could've easily chosen a song about my mama, but I had to choose something that would make her want to dance, like we did when we were back at home and she was burning her pine cones and sipping her wine.

My mama threw her arms up over her head and went wiggling her hips in her soft gold, silk dress that had some of my older employees about to get fucked up for staring too hard at her in it.

"Would you mind?" my mama sang, really enjoying the music.

I shimmied closer to her, stepping from side to side and twirling around, like we had done when I was younger. Where we were didn't matter. We were having a good time like we did way back then.

Finally, after kissing my mama's cheeks, it was time

for me to dance with my butterbean wife. The largest smile I had, had developed onto my face. Camaya shyly came over to me with such a shy smile that it made me want to take her hand and twirl her more than I planned to. Instead, I pulled her close while John Legend's voice filled the venue with the stylings of *All of Me*.

Together, we gently swayed from side to side with her head laying against my rib. I hadn't really paid attention to how much shorter Camaya was than me until now. I didn't have on shoes and she wasn't wearing heels. She was almost a wee woman compared to me. Then, a thought hit me.

"You remember when we first danced together?" I quietly asked to her.

She looked up at me with that innocent smile that had originally melted the ice around my heart that I had years ago. "You mean the night when you got lit, and ran away from me when Jamie Foxx was singing? Yeah, because I remember that night very well."

"I could feel some type of love for you on that night, and it was only the first day that you had been in my house."

"Really?"

"Really. I've never been smitten or ever believed in love at first sight. That was until the beauty met the beast."

"Shut up, Nas. I wasn't beautiful. I looked like a wet, blind mutt."

"To you. But to me, you were gorgeous, baby."

She blushed, resting her head against me again. "How'd you put all this together, with your extra slick self? Who made my dress?"

"Oh, Lucy made your dress. She's very good with her eyes, babe. I stole one of your maternity blouses for your measurements, and she did the damn thing. I think you should have her do a maternity line or something. The event itself was Laz's idea."

Her head sprung up to me.

"I thought he was crazy at first, but it worked. He felt like we should stop playing around and get it done. It took me a good month, but here we are. Married in secrecy and privacy."

"I love you so much, Nas."

"I love you too, Cammy. If I didn't, I wouldn't have been sweating bullets for the last thirty days when trying to put all this together."

"You were very slick with it." She giggled.

"Camaya, I never told you. It felt like I had been shot in the chest when I met you. I didn't know what it was. I was scared to let you in, I got overprotective of you because I didn't want you hurt again, even though I was hurting and helping at the same time. And then, I had to tell the truth to myself. I was in love with you before I even let it come out of my mouth. I'm so glad that you hung in there with me, baby. I'm sorry about everything. I know that I can't change the past, but I can most definitely be better in the future. That means that as submissive as you are to me, I promise to be as equally easy-going and cooperative."

"I believe you because if I divorce your ass, you're gonna be one broke motherfucker."

"You and this cussin'. I'm going to have to get used to it."

"Yes, you will. Along with the fact that if you fuck up, that's two payments of child support, plus spousal support. I feel bad for you, buddy."

"I'll give it all to you without having to fuck up. How about that?"

She lifted her chin, giving me a full view of those pretty lips that I loved to bite on when we were in the bedroom. "Give me that lovin', Mr. Asaad."

"I damn sure will, Mrs. Asaad."

We shared a deep kiss that lasted longer than the music had. With my world complete, I was walking on air. No weed, no money, no vacation would ever compare to me having the sweetest girl that ever came up out of the projects, the prettiest little rambunctious girl, and the chance of having a new baby to join it all.

***

Since I didn't get clearance from Camaya's doctor to travel for our honeymoon, I sent my mama on vacation instead, for a week, and took my daughter and wife back to our home, so we could enjoy the rest of our night as a family, officially by law. Because I had seen it in the movies, I carried Camaya over the threshold of our home, even though she had opposed because she thought she was too big, but with how I had been working out, I was able to.

Still in her gorgeous dress that Lucy did her thing with, we traveled up the steps, helped Abby to undress, and put her in the bed. We prayed over her, gave her Peppa Pig, and waited until she drifted off to sleep.

Camaya made a stop inside the room she chose for the nursery and stared inside for a moment. "Just a few more weeks, and our little one will be here," she said lowly.

I pecked her lips and pulled her by the hand into our bedroom. We showered together, where I couldn't stop kissing her belly or her ring. Still, I was high on love and life. It was very apparent that I was happy. Especially when I had to take advantage of my new wife by bending her over the shower bench to welcome her into our marriage.

When all was said and done, she slipped into her underwear and silk nightgown, while I pulled on a pair of briefs, leaving my pajama bottoms on the chest at the foot of our bed. Mrs. Asaad and I cuddled and made out like two love-sick teens before we finally dozed off.

With as happy as I was, I couldn't sleep. It seemed as if the atmosphere had shifted in my home. It dawned on me that I had forgotten to lock the house and set the alarm. How the fuck could I had been so forgetful when that was my nightly routine, even before we had gotten this house?

Carefully, I slipped my arm from under Camaya's head and eased out of bed so I wouldn't disturb her. Then I pulled on my pajama bottoms before leaving the room. I walked softly out of the room and into the hall. Just as I had walked past Abby's bedroom, I had to back up and look inside one more time. As a precaution, I turned on the light, finding that my daughter was not in her bed. Peppa Pig lay on the floor. *Red flag.* She carried that damn pig everywhere. I mean *everywhere.*

To be safe, I checked the hall bathroom, where the light was always on for her, yet she wasn't there. My heart fell out of my chest. I scurried back into the room to wake Camaya. There was no way that my daughter would even wander down the steps alone at this time of night, because

I always cut the light on the stairs off so she wouldn't try and go into the kitchen alone. If she was hungry or thirsty, she would always come to me and wake me so I could get whatever it was for her.

Camaya grumbled and stirred in her sleep. When she opened her eyes, she flinched.

I held my finger up to my lips for her to stay quiet, then pulled my wife out of bed. "Get under the bed and stay there," I whispered. "You remember where my guns are, don't you?"

She vigorously nodded with worry all over her beautiful face.

I left her there, taking the first set of steps, only stopping to reach inside a built-in shelf behind an elephant statue that Camaya had there. It wasn't the only concealed weapon in my home. Call me paranoid, but at times like these, you'd be happy to have me spend the night at your crib. I was always packing.

Quietly, I moved in the dark toward the base of the stairs. I could hear whispering from around the corner. A very familiar voice. The closer I got, I could tell that she

185

was singing *Ring Around the Rosie* in some choppy, raspy voice.

I touched the circular light switch behind me to turn it on at the bottom of the steps.

Donica gasped and turned to me. She had one arm around my scared daughter's shoulders, and her other hand was behind her back. I squinted at her. She was completely disheveled. Her hair was crazy and matted, and I could smell the bitch from where I was standing. Her lips were visibly chapped, her red dress was dirty, and she wasn't even wearing any shoes. Where she had come from, I didn't know. All I knew was that I wasn't stupid. She had to have a weapon in her hand or else Abigail Asaad would've screamed. She didn't too much like strangers. Especially strangers who were dirty.

I gave Donica an upwards nod. "'Sup?"

"Congratulations," she said. Her voice sounded as if it was about to give out on her at any given time. "Where's your pretty, fat fuck of a wife?"

"Why are you in my house, Donica? Why do you have my daughter?"

"You mean *our* daughter? And why am I in *our* house?"

"No. I meant what I said. Answer me."

"*You* answer *me!*"

"What do you want? My daughter needs to be in bed."

Her face cracked and formed a deep frown that I really didn't give a fuck about. "This was supposed to be mine," she cried. "Wasn't I good enough?"

"Are you high?"

"Answer me!"

"Donica, under the circumstances, you weren't who I wanted."

She straightened her face within the bat of a lash. "It had nothing to do with Camaya, did it? It was all because of this fucking brat? Wasn't it? You didn't give a fuck about me or Camaya's sloppy ass. You chased her for the girl. Admit it to me."

"I married my wife because I love her, alright? I was in love with her, but Abby was an incentive."

"Daddy, I'm scared," Abby whined.

Donica looked down at her with a smile. "Don't be scared, baby girl. I won't hurt you. I bet your daddy didn't tell you that I was supposed to be your mama, did he? No, he didn't. It's because he's a selfish asshole who doesn't give a fuck about anyone but himself. He doesn't care about the people he has to step on to get what he wants. No. He just does whatever the fuck he wants to do. Never mind the people who really love him."

"Donica, if you leave right now, I promise not to press charges," I told her sternly.

She looked at me as if I had lost my mind. There was a darkness behind her eyes.

I approached her, tapping my .357 against my leg. With every step I took, she backed up with my daughter still under her arm. I was facing my kitchen, with her back to it. "Let my daughter go."

Angry with me, she pulled her hand from behind her back, revealing her pistol. "Hand over the fucking gun, Nas," she demanded. "You hand it over, or else your precious daughter meets her maker. I don't give a fuck

188

about *me*. You might shoot me, but I will hang on until I see her little ass leaking."

"What is it you really want?"

"You got two options. Leave Camaya and be with me so we can raise our rightful child together, or I can kill everybody in this bitch, including me."

"Do you see how that wouldn't work out? I'd only be leaving her to live with you out of fear of death, not because I love you. It wouldn't be real."

"I don't give a damn. Make your choice."

"I could never be with you."

Without hesitating, she pulled the trigger, grazing my hand. I dropped my gun, just before I could hear another bang go off, ripping through my shoulder.

"Daddy!" Abby screeched.

Before I hit the floor, I saw Donica grab my daughter's hair and shove her head into the pillar next to my living room. Abby yelped, then her little body dropped unconsciously. I did my damnedest to reach for my gun, yet Donica kicked it away from me and took a step back so

I couldn't reach for her.

"Crawl to me, bitch," Donica said through grinding teeth.

"Kneel, hoe," I heard my wife say.

What sounded like thunder ripped through the room. Donica dropped to her knees and landed on her face.

Camaya ran over to Abby first, slapping her cheek to see if she would wake up. "Abby, baby!" she cried. "Come on, baby, wake up for mommy."

"Cam," I struggled to say.

She looked over at me on the floor with terror written all over her face. "Baby! Baby, hang on, okay? I called the police. Somebody should be here soon." She cradled our daughter in her arms, rocking with her with tears glossing her cheeks. "Nas, please!" she screamed. She could see that my eyes were getting lower.

Behind my lids, my vision was going blurry. I was losing a hell of a lot of blood. I knew so because I was getting cold.

"Baby, don't go!"

The door behind me was getting banged on. "Nas!" Meech screamed from the other side.

"Baby!"

"Nas! Camaya!"

"Baby, stay awake!"

The crash of my front door couldn't even get Abby awake or make me flinch. It was getting darker and colder.

with love and respect

Laconia Reneé

OTHER READS

Be sure to LIKE our Major Key

Publishing page on Facebook!

CPSIA information can be obtained
at www.ICGtesting.com
Printed in the USA
LVOW03s1738270218
568057LV00014B/1060/P